TARGET FIVE

(THE SPY GAME—BOOK 5)

JACK MARS

Jack Mars

Jack Mars is the USA Today bestselling author of the LUKE STONE thriller series, which includes seven books. He is also the author of the new FORGING OF LUKE STONE prequel series, comprising six books; of the AGENT ZERO spy thriller series, comprising twelve books; of the TROY STARK thriller series, comprising five books; and of the SPY GAME thriller series, comprising seven books.

Jack loves to hear from you, so please feel free to visit www.Jackmarsauthor.com to join the email list, receive a free book, receive free giveaways, connect on Facebook and Twitter, and stay in touch!

ISBN: 978-1-0943-8244-9

BOOKS BY JACK MARS

THE SPY GAME
TARGET ONE (Book #1)
TARGET TWO (Book #2)
TARGET THREE (Book #3)
TARGET FOUR (Book #4)
TARGET FIVE (Book #5)
TARGET SIX (Book #6)
TARGET SEVEN (Book #7)

TROY STARK THRILLER SERIES
ROGUE FORCE (Book #1)
ROGUE COMMAND (Book #2)
ROGUE TARGET (Book #3)
ROGUE MISSION (Book #4)
ROGUE SHOT (Book #5)

LUKE STONE THRILLER SERIES
ANY MEANS NECESSARY (Book #1)
OATH OF OFFICE (Book #2)
SITUATION ROOM (Book #3)
OPPOSE ANY FOE (Book #4)
PRESIDENT ELECT (Book #5)
OUR SACRED HONOR (Book #6)
HOUSE DIVIDED (Book #7)

FORGING OF LUKE STONE PREQUEL SERIES
PRIMARY TARGET (Book #1)
PRIMARY COMMAND (Book #2)
PRIMARY THREAT (Book #3)
PRIMARY GLORY (Book #4)
PRIMARY VALOR (Book #5)
PRIMARY DUTY (Book #6)

AN AGENT ZERO SPY THRILLER SERIES
AGENT ZERO (Book #1)
TARGET ZERO (Book #2)
HUNTING ZERO (Book #3)

TRAPPING ZERO (Book #4)
FILE ZERO (Book #5)
RECALL ZERO (Book #6)
ASSASSIN ZERO (Book #7)
DECOY ZERO (Book #8)
CHASING ZERO (Book #9)
VENGEANCE ZERO (Book #10)
ZERO ZERO (Book #11)
ABSOLUTE ZERO (Book #12)

PROLOGUE

Northwest Balochistan Province, Pakistan
Near the borders of Iran and Afghanistan
Early evening

Robert Murphy steered the drone out of the darkening sky and back down to Earth, using the joystick and button controls to bring it to a soft landing precisely at his feet. Another day was done, and another night of being on constant guard for danger was about to start.

He spared a glance around the archaeological site, a dusty stretch of hilltop where ancient foundations made of heavy blocks stuck out of the topsoil here and there. A test trench ran through the center of the site, expanded at three points into excavation squares measuring two meters to a side. His crew had excavated two more squares in outlying spots. At the more distant one, Robert saw Oscar Dortmund, his second in command, finishing up work.

It was almost time for evening prayer when the muezzin at the mosque in the valley would turn on the minaret's loudspeaker with a loud screech of feedback, cough fifty years of cigarettes into the mic, and then launch into a lilting, pitch-perfect recitation of the call to prayer. That would come in a few minutes. By then, the field crew of ten local workers would have covered the trench and squares with tarps, stowed their tools in the lockup at the edge of the site, and started down the narrow path cutting along the side of the hill to the village where they lived, first to pray in the mosque, and then go into one of the stout stone houses that made up Zaranka, a village a couple thousand souls.

Robert, Oscar, and Nadeem, the Pakistani foreman, would go the other way to a large farmhouse they had rented from a local family, paying them more than the profit from the upcoming harvest to move to their cousin's house in town for the three months of the excavation. He could see Nadeem strolling over, having dismissed his section of the crew. They had finished a couple of minutes early. Efficient guy, Nadeem. Smart too. Too damn efficient and smart.

Nadeem was only twenty-four, the son of a gold cloth merchant who had decided to go the academic route and became a graduate student in archaeology at the University of Islamabad.

The kid, Robert, was only fifteen years older, but his experience made anyone that young feel like a kid—he sure knew his stuff. He'd caught out Robert in a couple of lapses of knowledge already.

Robert passed that off to feeling "tired from the heat," pretending to be affected by northwest Pakistan's harsh weather when in fact, he'd been doing missions in Latin American jungles for years. Or he'd apologize and say that "my bad Urdu made me misunderstand," even though he was fluent in the language and had to focus on every conversation to insert mistakes in his grammar and occasionally ask for words he actually knew.

Nadeem just laughed at these excuses and said, "Oh, your Urdu is very good, Professor Murphy, very good. And your knowledge of my country's past is truly impressive."

That was more South Asian hospitality than the actual truth. Robert could tell Nadeem had begun to harbor doubts, which was why he grew extra suspicious as he saw Nadeem wearing a light brown *shalwar kameez* and a darker brown wool *pakol*, the soft cap with the rolled-up brim worn by most men in the region, strolling across the site and headed right for him. The younger man with the wire-rimmed glasses and university education was all curiosity and enthusiasm. They should have never picked him for dig foreman.

Nadeem was way too interested in the drone. Sure, it was technology he didn't have access to at his university, but the novelty should have worn off by now.

Robert stuck a pen drive into a slot in the drone's undercarriage. The drone had been programmed to wipe out any film from its memory when it transferred it to an external drive. It was safer that way.

"Nadeem, could you come look at this square?" Oscar called from the other side of the site. "I need a second opinion on this feature."

Good job, Oscar.

Robert fidgeted as the thumb drive finished downloading—a long process because two hours of high-resolution imagery takes up a lot of storage space—and managed a friendly wave as the last group of workers bade farewell to the foreigners and the educated Pakistani from the big city and headed down to the village of Zaranka, where their families had lived for uncounted generations.

Oscar kept Nadeem busy as the downloading finished. Once it was done and the drone's memory was cleaned, if the Pakistani graduate student got too nosey and connected the drone to a laptop to look at the files, all he'd see would be a standard survey pattern of the next valley to the north, film that Robert had taken a week ago but which constantly updated its time stamp to make any unfamiliar eyes think was taken that day.

The thumb drive flashed green, and Robert yanked it out, ready to put it in his pocket. Then the low rumble of an approaching engine came to his ears.

He stood and looked around. On the path to the village, just passing the crew as they went downhill, came three Pakistani army Humvees trundling up the hill, coming towards them.

Oh, crap.

Robert looked around, desperate to find a place to hide the thumb drive.

The nearest excavation square, now covered with a tarpaulin, contained a wall with a frieze of dancing figures along with an inscription in Harappan script, their best discovery so far, he supposed.

Robert Murphy didn't really know much about archaeology beyond how to fake it. But from what he'd read and what their far more knowledgeable foreman had mentioned, this was a site on the frontier of the Indus Valley civilization that prospered more than four thousand years ago.

Getting on his hands and knees so he couldn't be seen from the vehicles coming up the slope, he scrambled over to the square, lifted the tarp, and shoved the thumb drive into a narrow space between the earth and the frieze. Then he replaced the tarp, glanced over at Oscar and Nadeem to see them staring at the Humvees, and stood.

The three army vehicles were almost to the top. He could see they were full of soldiers.

Putting on an innocent smile, Robert strode toward them and waved.

The Hummers bounced up the last stretch of rocky slope and came to a halt right in front of them, spitting grit and dust into Robert's face. They idled, all in a row. For a moment, no one got out. Beyond the Hummers, the field crew had stopped and stared from a safe distance. In this border region of Pakistan, the arrival of the military was never good news. He glanced to his left and saw Oscar wearing a smile he knew wasn't genuine and Nadeem wearing a very honest worried expression.

Then all the doors to all three Hummers opened at the same time. Soldiers got out in full battle gear, with helmets, Kevlar, and PK-21 assault rifles, a local version of the Russian AK-103. Not the best assault rifles on the market, but deadly enough.

The soldiers appeared alert but at ease. That did not reassure Robert Murphy.

Once the fifteen troops had arrayed themselves in a rough line along the edge of the hill, they gestured for Oscar and Nadeem to come closer. Reluctantly, they did.

A sergeant stepped forward and addressed Nadeem: "Tell the foreigners that we must search them," he said in Urdu.

"I speak your language," Robert said.

"Very well. Are you in charge of this excavation?"

"Yes, I'm Dr. Richard Murton of Yale University," he said, giving both his false name and false accreditation.

"We must search you for security reasons."

"Mind telling me what this is all about?" Robert asked, raising his arms up so a private could frisk him. Two more frisked Oscar and Nadeem.

"The colonel will tell you," the sergeant said.

Once they had all been frisked, a door to the third Hummer opened, and an older man with salt and pepper hair under his beret got out. He carried only a sidearm and an air of authority. The sergeant turned and saluted.

"Nothing on them, sir."

The colonel nodded, then turned to Robert and addressed him in heavily accented English.

"You are all under arrest."

Nadeem gasped and tried to choke out a protest. Robert and Oscar took on confused looks as if they didn't know exactly what this was all about.

How did they find out? Was I too obvious with the drone? Did they have trained spotters watching out for it?

Damn, I knew it was a risk. Not that there was any other way to gather the intel we needed.

"Arrested?" Robert sputtered in his best imitation of hurt innocence. "We have a permit to dig on this site. We've been here for weeks!"

The colonel's eyes narrowed. "If you are archaeologists then I am the king of England." He pointed at the drone sitting like a metallic insect nearby. "Would you explain what you were doing with that?"

"We use drones to conduct aerial surveys of the region to look for more ancient sites."

The colonel stared at him a moment. Robert wondered if his English hadn't been equal to understanding that sentence.

Turned out his English was better than Robert supposed. "We have been monitoring your drone for several days now. It hasn't been searching in a regimented pattern as you would do if you were looking for archaeological sites. Instead, you've been sending it far out, miles and miles away from here and high up enough that you hoped it wouldn't be spotted, or putting it between the targets and the rising and setting sun."

"Targets?" Robert asked, still feigning surprise.

"Sensitive military sites," the colonel snapped.

Nadeem gasped and stared at Robert—his face showed shock, denial, and then suspicion. Robert looked away from his foreman and back at his interrogator.

"We haven't filmed any military sites." *Only terrorist training camps.* "Check the drone footage yourself."

"We will do that, but what the footage shows is of lesser importance. It can be faked. You most certainly did have it go on regular search patterns at some times to mask your real intentions. I suspect when we look through the drone's memory that is all we will find. But we will find the other footage. Even if we don't, we know where the drone has been going. We've had spotters on several of hilltops with powerful binoculars watching it."

And I never saw them through the drone's camera? These guys are good.

The colonel nodded to one of the privates, who moved forward and handcuffed Oscar.

Briefly, Robert thought of running, an instinctive fight or flight response that was, of course, foolhardy. He stayed where he was.

"As American citizens, we have a right to speak with our embassy."

"Spies have no rights." The colonel looked at Nadeem and spat. "And as for this traitor, he has even less than you do."

The private with the handcuffs gave Nadeem a wicked smile. The foreman paled and meekly held out his hands to be handcuffed.

Robert's heart sank. There might still be a way out of this for himself and his partner, but their poor, innocent graduate student was in for a world of suffering. And if the Pakistani government discovered the truth about their mission, he and Oscar would end up in front of a firing squad.

CHAPTER ONE

A back alley in Tetouan, northern Morocco
That same day ...

Jana Peters was getting tired of pretending to be interested in tourist junk. What was taking Jacob so long?

She stood in a narrow alley in the labyrinth of almost identical alleys spreading out behind the royal palace in Tetouan's medieval old city. It was a narrow, sunless place of blank walls punctuated only by a few tightly shuttered windows high out of reach. The alley was some distance from the wider, busier alleys, and there wasn't much tourist traffic, only a few local women walking along with heavy canvas shopping bags of fruit and vegetables, the bottoms of their faces covered with white cloth *haiks*. A few men walked by as well, looking almost Biblical in brown hooded djellabas. They strolled along in pairs, speaking quietly to themselves in the reserved manner of Moroccans, or walked along, intent on some task.

Jana kept an eye on all of them, as well as on the shut door opposite the tourist shop. It was a tough thing to do since the shop owner was intent on dangling every cheap trinket in Morocco in front of her face. His supply of tasteless trash seemed limitless.

"How about this beautiful camel, madam?" the pot-bellied man in the blue djellaba said, holding out a camel doll about a foot long. It gave off a foul smell, almost as bad as the real thing. She wondered what it was stuffed with.

"Oh, I just can't decide what to buy my niece and nephew."

"We have very fine jewelry, madam. Your niece love very much. Come. Let me show you case inside."

The shopkeeper had been trying to lure her inside to look at more of his "treasures," including a dusty old glass case in the dark back region of his shop, which was a little bigger than a walk-in closet.

"Oh, let me look at more things out here." Jana pretended to be nervous about going inside with him. She needed to stay out here where she could monitor the situation.

She wasn't worried about the guy. His eye movements showed he wasn't a lookout for that door across the alley, and he wasn't checking her out more than any regular man did, even though she was wearing a T-shirt and shorts like a tourist instead of the more conservative clothing she regularly wore in this Muslim nation. Besides, if he tried anything, her self-defense training and the 9mm automatic in her purse would make short work of him.

"Let me bring the treasures to you, madam," he said, trying a different tactic.

He bustled over to the case and started fiddling with a key to open it, muttering to himself in Arabic about the stubbornness of foreign women being almost equal to the stubbornness of the rusted old lock.

Jana took the opportunity to look around the alley. The door across the way and a few steps to her right remained closed, a blank face of green-painted metal.

Jacob Snow was in there, speaking to a former CIA informant who had broken ties with the organization because of a fight over payment. Jacob said that didn't sound realistic since the informant had been paid well. The real reason for the rift remained a mystery. Going to this guy was a risk, but he was knowledgeable, had ties to Central Asia, and might just have an idea where her father was.

Aaron Peters had been the CIA's greatest operative until he got killed in an explosion in Raqqah, the capital of the Islamic State. He and Jacob had taken out one of ISIS's main ammunition dumps, but her dad hadn't gotten out alive. At least that was the official story, which Jacob and Jana had both believed until a strange message in a code only her father and Jacob knew warned of Jana's abduction by The Order, a shadowy organization at odds with Western democracy. That tipoff had saved her life and made them both wonder.

Was Aaron Peters still alive? It hardly seemed credible, and yet what other explanation was there? Aaron had told Jacob, his protégé, that he would never reveal the code to anyone else and made Jacob swear the same. Why would he have gone back on his word when such a thing might endanger himself, his daughter, and Jacob? So here they were in Tetouan, looking for answers. And she was looking out for trouble. Because trouble could come in all forms on a mission like this.

She scanned the Moroccans, both the men and the women, looking for familiar faces or suspicious activity. The only familiar face she saw was that of Ghanem ibn Tariq, an agent from the Moroccan secret service attached to this mission, and she barely saw him at all. An expert at covert surveillance, he had changed clothing twice already in the past half hour, lost a fake mustache and gained a fake scar, and was passing through the neighborhood for the third time at least. Jana couldn't be sure he hadn't passed by other times without her spotting him. He was that good.

She looked up and down the alley—in one direction, it made a right turn after a few yards with a cloth merchant on the corner; in the other direction, it ran straight for a good hundred yards before angling off out of sight—and didn't spot anyone else acting strangely. Wait, except for that stout older Moroccan in Western garb. He stood about thirty yards away, occasionally blocked by other pedestrians, fiddling with his phone.

From her vantage point, she couldn't see anything close to him, but she estimated him to be standing just outside the entrance to a dingy café that was at about that spot.

Suspicious? Maybe. Moroccan buildings had thick walls, and he might not be able to get a signal inside the café, although most cafes had WiFi these days.

The guy seemed a bit off, though. He wasn't staring as intently at his phone as people usually did, and few people in this neighborhood dressed in Western styles.

Ghanem ibn Tariq had already passed her. Too bad. She would have liked to have given him a signal. Knowing Ghanem, however, he had scoped the guy out already.

"Look at this, madam! Treasures of the East!"

The shopkeeper dangled some fake gold necklaces in front of her and one tarnished chain that might actually have been real silver.

"Oh, and I have ancient coins too. Would you like to see them? Very old."

That aroused a flicker of interest. As an archaeologist, she couldn't resist looking at actual antiquities, which these cheap necklaces most certainly were not.

"Sure," she said.

He disappeared into the back of his shop again, and Jana, holding up a bright yellow scarf as if examining it, scanned the long section of the alley once more.

Mr. Cell Phone was still fiddling. Ghanem was approaching him now. Three more men and two women were also in view. Only two pedestrians, a man and a woman walking together, were heading in her direction.

She looked the other way and saw no one except for the cloth merchant standing in the doorway of his shop, smoking a cigarette and looking sleepy.

"Here, look at these treasures, madam!"

The shopkeeper's voice carried a note of desperation. She had been browsing his shop for way too long without buying anything. What was keeping Jacob so long?

"Fine coins, madam. Very ancient."

She looked at them. One was a battered old coin from the 1950s when Morocco had become an independent nation, another was a lump of bronze with the face so abraded she couldn't tell what it had once been, and the third was a poor imitation of a Roman denarius made of aluminum. Aluminum! Did the Romans have soda cans too? She was tempted to buy it just so she could get a good laugh at archaeology conferences, then decided she couldn't reward such behavior.

"Ah, I see you like the Roman coin, madam. You have good eye. For you special price."

"It sure is … unique."

"Yes, it is very much a special piece. I—"

The shopkeeper's patter broke off as three gunshots rang out in rapid succession, echoing dully down the confines of the alley. They sounded muted as if coming from behind that green metal door.

"What was that?" the shopkeeper cried in Arabic, forgetting in his shock that he was speaking to someone who supposedly didn't understand the language.

Everyone in the alley turned and stared. The guy with the cell phone put it in his pocket.

A moment later, the green door opened, and a thin, wiry Moroccan man in jeans, a dress shirt, a leather jacket, and a baseball cap with a brim pulled low over his face burst out and sprinted down the alley, heading the short way for the nearby right turn. That would bring him right past her.

Despite his effort to hide his features, Jana recognized Roschdy Qissi, the former informant, from a file photo Jacob had shown her.

Roschdy sprinted down the alley. Just as he passed, Jana put out a leg to trip him.

The guy was too quick. He leaped over her leg and smacked an elbow into her face. Jana slammed against the doorway to the shop, hurting her back on the angle of the stonework. She staggered into the alley as several people cried out in shock.

As she managed to focus, she saw the informant round the corner and disappear. The cloth merchant stared, his cigarette falling out of his gaping mouth.

Jana glanced at the open doorway to the informant's hideout. Pursue or go check on Jacob?

Ghanem had disappeared. She had no backup. She decided that help would come for Jacob soon enough in this crowded neighborhood, and if he was hurt, there wasn't much she could do for him. She went after Roschdy.

Rounding the corner, she saw him well ahead, running straight down a narrow alley, having passed one side alley already. A couple of passersby had stopped to stare.

Was he hurrying toward a particular destination? Why not go down that side alley and disappear? Maybe it was a dead end. There were a lot of them in the medinas of North Africa.

Roschdy glanced over his shoulder and saw her in pursuit. He reached into his leather jacket.

Jana stopped, got to one knee, and pulled out her pistol. The onlookers screamed and dove into a doorway.

Roschdy tossed a small metal sphere down the alley in her direction. Because he didn't slow down, his aim was off, and it clinked off one wall to land short.

Not short enough. Jana cursed and threw herself into a doorway, hoping the three inches that the doorway was inset from the wall would somehow miraculously shield her from all the shrapnel.

CHAPTER TWO

The grenade detonated, but not as loudly as she thought it would.

Jana dared a peek and saw a yellowish cloud filling the alley, obscuring her view of the runaway informant.

Tear gas? She had to risk it. Jana held her breath, shut her eyes, and ran down the alley, keeping her arms splayed so she didn't veer off course and hit a wall. She didn't. Instead, she tripped over what felt like a body and did a faceplant on the gritty earth. As she impacted, the air got knocked from her lungs, and she automatically sucked in a bit of the acrid gas. Jana stopped herself from breathing in more. Lungs burning, eyes still screwed shut, she crawled forward far enough that she hoped she was out of the cloud. By now, her lungs felt like they were on fire. They had no oxygen in them, only a whiff of tear gas. She coughed and coughed again as she tried to stand, then sucked in a deep breath. The air was thankfully clean. She exhaled and opened her eyes as she took another breath… and instantly regretted it. The cloud was expanding, and its tenuous edge had reached her position to give her a second sampling of tear gas. It wasn't much, just enough to send her into another coughing fit and make her eyes water.

She staggered forward, wiping her eyes, desperate to get some good, clean air.

After a moment, she recovered enough to see that the informant had vanished. Jana cursed and ran forward, her lungs burning, every breath coming out as the tortured wheeze of a lifelong chain smoker. Through eyes still welling with tears, she spotted three terrified Moroccans sheltering in a *bakal*, one of the countless little hole-in-the-wall convenience stores that dotted every medina in the country. The shopkeeper and an older couple peeked over a narrow counter displaying cartons of milk, candy, and cleaning supplies.

"Which way did he go?" Jana rasped in Arabic.

All three ducked down behind the counter like a trio of reverse Jack-in-the-Boxes. Jana continued, her 9mm at the ready. She had somehow managed to keep hold of it despite getting teargassed.

Dad would be proud, she thought.

She came to a side alley she hadn't noticed before, hidden by a slight bend in the alley she was on. Jana swung around the corner, gun leveled, to find it was twenty yards long before coming to a turn. Someone darted around the far corner, too fast to see who it was. The informant or a fleeing pedestrian? She ran after them, still wheezing.

She came to the corner, got to one knee in case the guy was waiting to spring a nasty surprise, and peeked, leading with her gun. There was a long straightaway, and the informant was running for all he was worth.

Jana hesitated. With her eyes still tearing up and her breath coming ragged, if she tried to shoot the guy in the legs, she might miss or, even worse, hit him in the head. She couldn't kill someone who wasn't trying to kill her. Besides, she needed this guy alive.

She rose and continued the pursuit. Her lungs told her she wasn't up to the challenge, that the informant would lose her at the next twist and turn of Tetouan's labyrinthine alleyways.

Just then, Ghanem burst out of a side alley and tackled him, slamming him against the far wall. The two went down, the agent of the Moroccan secret service landing on top of the informant.

Where the hell did he come from?

Her dad always said to rely on the local talent. They knew the terrain much better. It would have taken Jana weeks, if not months, to learn all the alleyways in this city.

The informant struggled, so Ghanem gave him a hard punch to the face, twisted his arm, and flipped him onto his front.

Just as he was putting a knee into the informant's lower back and reaching into his pocket, probably for a zip cuff, a huge man wearing a hooded robe came out of the side alley. He reached into his voluminous sleeve and withdrew a wicked-looking dagger.

"Look out!" Jana shouted.

Ghanem looked up, saw the danger immediately, and sprang away. But he would not get away in time. The officer was on his knees, and the newcomer was towering over him. It was up to Jana.

She fired.

Chest still heaving, eyes still watering, she dared a shot with a pistol at twenty yards against one of three closely packed individuals.

Miraculously, she hit, taking the man in the right shoulder. He staggered back, dropping his knife.

Jana rose and paced forward.

"Don't make a move or I'll shoot to kill!" she shouted in Arabic.

Actually, she had been shooting to kill before, aiming for the man's center mass, but her aim was so off she hit him in the shoulder instead.

The informant had half risen. He looked at the foreign woman, whose red eyes and wheezing breath made her look like some sort of demon, and decided not to make a run for it. Ghanem threw him back down on the ground, secured his hands behind his back with zip cuffs, then pulled out a handheld radio to call for backup.

Jana made it to their position, keeping her gun trained on the giant man she had shot, who leaned against the alley wall clutching his shoulder and looking pale.

"What did you do to Jacob?" she asked the informant.

The man—a ratty-looking little fellow now that Jana got a good look at him—gave her a nasty grin.

"I plugged your friend. I'd like to plug everyone in the CIA if I got the chance."

"You failed at that like you failed at everything else," a voice from the side alley said.

Everyone turned and saw Jacob walking toward them, the left side of his shirt soaked with blood. The red stain ran down his left leg, and Jana could swear she heard a soft squishing sound as he took each step.

"You okay?" Jana said, coming up to him. A stupid question for anyone except Jacob. He'd been in far worse shape and come out on top.

"Keep an eye on the prisoners," he said, making Jana remember to turn and point her gun back at the knifeman. He hadn't budged throughout the couple of seconds she had taken her eyes off him. That bullet had taken the fight out of him.

"Are you all right?" Jana asked again.

"Oh, just fine and dandy."

"You're bleeding like a stuck pig, my friend," Ghanem said in English, moving over to the second prisoner to zip-cuff his wrists.

"Pigs are *haram* in Islam," Jacob said. "Don't compare me to a pig."

"It's an American expression I learned at a Special Forces training camp down in Virginia. And don't tell me you don't eat bacon and drink alcohol, because you do. You're about as Muslim as the Spice Girls."

"Quit joking around and call someone to patch me up," Jacob grunted.

Ghanem got on the radio and called for medical personnel. Just then, a pair of uniformed policemen came running up. Ghanem flashed a badge, and they saluted.

"Take these two prisoners, give them medical treatment, and prepare them for questioning."

Jacob gazed down at the informant. "Hear that, buddy? You're getting prepared for questioning, and in a Moroccan police station, that means you're in for a lot more pain than you inflicted on me."

***

Jacob had been bluffing about the torture. He knew Roschdy Qissi, the informant, well enough to know that it wouldn't be necessary, and Jacob only authorized it in his presence in the direst of circumstances, like once when a bomb in Nigeria was due to go off and a member of the radical group Boko Haram was in the sweatbox of the local police station. The Nigerian police had done terrible things to him, and Jacob had stood by and not intervened, but in the end, they had learned where the bomb was hidden under a stall at the local marketplace. Defusing it must have saved at least twenty or thirty lives. When you played in rough parts of the world, sometimes you had to play rough.

Not with Roschdy Qissi. As soon as he saw the inside of a prison cell and the three burly cops Jacob had acted like they were limbering up for the mother of all beatdowns, he sang like a canary.

Now Jacob sat, freshly bandaged with his side singing with pain, in an interrogation room facing Roschdy. The trio of bullies in uniform loomed behind him. One kept cracking his knuckles, a sound like pistol shots in the confines of the little concrete room.

"So you're ready to talk?" Jacob asked.

"Yeah. I didn't mean to shoot you."

"Riiiight. You aimed a gun at me and fired completely by accident."

"I thought you'd been sent to take me out."

"Why would you think that, Roschdy?"

"Because I stopped giving you information. The heat was getting too much. Some people, some pretty nasty people, started asking too many questions. Not every CIA agent who comes through here is as careful as you. Some were spotted, and people wanted to know why I was meeting in secret with so many foreigners."

"Didn't you explain that it was part of your import/export business?"

The guy imported guns and exported drugs. A fine, upstanding citizen. In the CIA, sometimes you had to make alliances with lesser evils to take out greater ones.

Roschdy shook his head. "I got taken out of that business. The local gangs pushed me out of it. Now I don't have any way to make money."

"Oh, so that's why you demanded five grand just to talk to me."

He shrugged his narrow shoulders. "Business is business."

Jacob leaned forward, the graze in his side aching from the movement. "Well, here's a business proposition for you. I need to know about an old contact of yours. I don't know what name he gave you, but it was a fake one."

"Of course." Roschdy Qissi shrugged like Jacob was saying the obvious, which he was.

Jacob went on. "If you give us information that leads us to this man, you'll see the sunlight again. If not … "

The CIA operative didn't need to finish his sentence. Roschdy had seen the inside of a Moroccan prison before, and no man who had ever done that wanted to repeat the experience.

"What about Mahmoud?" Roschdy asked.

"Your backup man with the big knife? He's not part of the deal. He does his time like a good boy. You have a chance to go a different way."

"Tell me about this man you're looking for," Roschdy said without hesitation. It was like Mahmoud no longer existed.

Jacob pulled out a photo of Aaron Peters. The informant studied it. No recognition sparked in his eyes, but they did narrow a bit.

Trying to think of a good story, eh?

"You only get released if we find him. Not before."

Roschdy twisted his mouth like he had tasted something bitter. "I haven't seen him before."

"How about this man?" Jacob pulled out another photo. It was of Sydney Franke, Aaron's longtime partner. They often worked on missions together and went way back. But like with any other partnership in the CIA, it was subject to the whims of the higher-ups. They had spent as much time working apart, not knowing each other's actions or locations as they did together. When Aaron and Jacob busted into Raqqa all those years ago, Franke had been on assignment in a different hotspot.

Jacob hadn't seen Sydney in years, and his boss wouldn't reveal where he was, but he'd heard through the grapevine that he was in Morocco. If anyone knew more about Aaron Peters than Jacob, it would be Sydney Franke.

Roschdy's eyes lit up. "I know that guy! He's been here for a couple of months. Before that he was in Taroudant."

"Taroudant?" That was a city south of the Atlas.

"Some jihadists have been trying to recruit there," Roschdy told him. "He was probably down there disrupting their operations. I presume he's CIA like you?"

"Never mind what he is. Just tell me where he is."

"Will this get me released?"

"If we find him, yes."

"He's got a safehouse deep in the medina. Sometimes another Western man joins him. I'll give you directions."

Jacob smiled and patted him on the shoulder. "Wouldn't it have been much easier if you had just given me this intel in the first place?"

"I thought you were trying to kill me."

"I'm sure I'm not the first. Let me tell you what, Roschdy. No hard feelings. If this intel turns out to be correct, you get to walk out of here and keep the money I gave you. That will be enough to get far away from here and set up somewhere else. After tossing a tear gas grenade in the medina and sending a knife-wielding maniac against a member of the Moroccan secret service, you're *persona non grata* in Tetouan." Jacob leaned forward. "But if this so-called safehouse turns out to be a dead lead, or a trap, you're going to never see daylight again."

The cop cracked his knuckles again. Roschdy looked over his shoulder and gulped.

CHAPTER THREE

Jacob studied the dead-end alley. Like many of the more prosperous cul-de-sacs in the medina, it ended in a tiny square no more than five paces to the side and fronted by four front doors to different homes. A locked gate sealed it off from the rest of the alley. There was no way to climb the thin metal mesh that ran between the heavy iron bars, and even if he could scale the ten feet up, a series of sharp spikes would make climbing over potentially hazardous to his manhood.

It didn't matter. Ghanem ibn Tariq was with him, and there was no lock in the world he couldn't pick.

Jana Peters was with him, too, standing close by his side as they peeked around the corner at the cul-de-sac. She trembled slightly. Jacob suspected that he was, too, although he was so keyed up he couldn't notice.

The impossible might lie beyond that gate. Aaron Peters might still be alive. He might even be in that house. The informant said a second Western man came in sometimes.

More likely, Sydney Franke was there. If he was, he might be able to explain the mystery of how Aaron had sent vital intel from beyond the grave.

The Moroccan secret service had done some background on this property and discovered it was owned by a Frenchman who lived in Marseilles and only occasionally traveled to Morocco. When he wasn't around, he rented it out as an Airbnb.

A common enough practice for both locals and expats, but neither Jacob nor his Moroccan colleagues bought that story for a second. This was a front. They hadn't found any information on the Frenchman, and the Airbnb website said the house was fully booked for six months. The reviews sounded fake, too, most of them being from users who hadn't posted reviews for any other properties.

The Moroccans had sent a request to the French secret service for further information on the landlord but so far hadn't heard back. The bureaucratic wheels in Paris turned slowly, and after all, it had only been six hours since they had gotten the address from Roschdy Qissi.

"Do you really think he could be in there?" Jana whispered.

"I don't know," Jacob replied, hearing his words come out shaky. "A fit middle-aged Western man was in there as recently as yesterday morning. A neighborhood informant told Ghanem."

"Morocco and its neighborhood informants," Jana muttered, shaking her head.

Like most Middle Eastern nations, the law relied on a vast network of paid informants to keep order and root out terrorists, dissidents, and criminals. They also kept their eyes on foreigners, both to make sure they weren't up to no good and to keep them safe from locals wishing to do them harm.

It worked, most of the time. Of course, those up to no good often had deep pockets and were more generous than the government. Paid informants weren't the best source of intel, but they were usually better than nothing. Usually.

If it really was Sydney or Aaron in there, he would have outwitted the informers or paid them off. And there was another mystery and another problem. The CIA couldn't tell him where Sydney was because it was classified. All it had told Jacob was that he was unavailable.

In CIA lingo, an agent being "unavailable" to speak with another agent could mean anything from the guy being dead to being too busy to the higher-ups having some reason for not wanting the two agents to speak with one another.

So Jacob hadn't mentioned this little nighttime call on his colleague to anyone else in the CIA. He also failed to mention to his Moroccan comrades that this wasn't authorized. What they didn't know couldn't get them in trouble.

This whole self-assigned mission was dangerous and potentially career-destroying, but he had to find answers. Had to find them almost as much as this amazing woman standing beside him. She'd lost her father to the CIA and deserved to know the truth. She deserved closure, closure her own government couldn't be bothered to give her.

Or him. What if Aaron really did survive Raqqa, as unbelievable as that was? They both deserved to know.

Ghanem took a final look around and walked up to the gate as casually as if he lived in the cul-de-sac. He wore a hooded djellaba that hid his features. As he got to the gate, he pulled out a lockpick from his pocket, fiddled for a moment, and the gate clicked open.

It was all done so quickly and in such a relaxed manner that a casual observer would have thought he had used a key.

Ghanem slipped inside. Jacob found himself hesitating. Jana hadn't moved either. Without looking at each other, they sought out each other's hand, grasped it, and walked through the gate together.

They had been hunting for Aaron Peters for a few weeks now, calling up old colleagues, tracking down leads that went nowhere, teasing out clues from Aaron's eventful but deeply secretive life. All this had led to a little cul-de-sac in northern Morocco and a break-in to a home that may hold the answers they needed.

Or yet another dead end.

Jacob's gaze darted all around them. The houses stood three or four stories tall, with shuttered windows like closed eyes. The whitewashed walls shone in the moonlight. They didn't hear a sound. It was still early, and some people in those houses would still be up, but Moroccan homes are private places, the shutters closing off all light, the thick walls muffling all sound. They were surrounded by people and yet seemed alone. Jacob scanned the rooftops to make sure no one was watching.

Ghanem moved over to the door and, with quick, relaxed movements, picked both locks in less than a minute, easing the locks open as quietly as he could.

Now came the tricky part. If someone was home, the door would be bolted, with no lock to pick to allow them access. Everyone bolted their doors in Morocco, and a man on a covert mission would certainly be no exception.

If no one was home, they could slip inside and investigate. If someone was home, then they'd simply have to knock and try to get them to talk.

And given the secretive nature of the occupant and the fact that the suspicious French landlord wasn't on any CIA contact list for this region, the prospect of an open conversation seemed unlikely.

Ghanem tried the door. It shifted a fraction of an inch, just enough to prove it wasn't bolted. He didn't open it further.

Relief and disappointment rushed through Jacob Snow's heart as he traded glances with Jana. They needed answers, and the house's shadowy occupant wasn't around to provide them. Maybe he was out for some reason.

Everyone paused.

"What if it's booby trapped?" Ghanem said.

"It won't be. Not our style."

Ghanem clicked his tongue. "We don't know this man's style."

Jana pushed between the two men and shoved open the door. Despite Jacob's confidence that it was safe, he found himself hissing through clenched teeth as the door opened.

Nothing. All was dark inside.

Jana slipped silently into the house. After a final look around, Jacob followed. Ghanem moved away to take a position as a sentry at the entrance to the dead-end alley.

They closed the door behind them, and each switched on a narrow-beamed flashlight. Shining them around, Jacob and Jana found themselves in a small entryway, a closed door leading to the rest of the house. Another bit of Moroccan privacy. The door to the street never gives a view inside the house.

Jacob checked for any tripwires, saw none, and opened the door. It led to a typical Moroccan living room. Their flashlights picked out low couches running along two walls. A large round table of hammered brass stood in the center. Jacob saw no personal items. The stairs led upwards.

They made a quick sweep of the rest of the house—the second floor with its two bedrooms and dining room, the upper floor with the kitchen and pantry. Nothing. No people and no sign of occupation. Jacob checked the refrigerator. The milk smelled okay, but the produce in the crisper had wilted and turned black. A narrow staircase led from the upper landing up to the roof. Jacob made his way up there and unbolted the door.

The screech of metal on metal would have been heard in every neighboring house.

Jacob gritted his teeth. People in the medina became intimately familiar with every sound. Anyone within earshot would know that the door to the roof had been opened in a supposedly unoccupied house.

Maybe that wasn't a bad thing. It could be interesting to see if anyone came to investigate.

The door opened with the creak of rusty hinges. Sydney or Aaron really should have oiled these. An unacceptable oversight. Then again, they probably never came up here. Too easy to be spotted or sniped at.

Moroccan roofs were often used by women during the day and the whole family at night. Jacob switched off his flashlight and crawled through the doorway so he wouldn't be seen from any neighboring rooftops.

He found a typical rooftop for the region with a waist-high wall around all four sides, a sunshade, and a few chairs. A clothesline ran from a PVC pipe set into the wall, sloping up slightly to the top of the little rooftop over the doorway.

Jacob paused, studying the clothesline. Instead of string, it was made of copper wire. He crouched down and studied the bottom of the doorway. Just as he suspected, a little notch had been filed into the metal of the door right at the bottom. A quick scan of the stars revealed that the wire ran north to south. It looked to be about five meters long. Actually, Jacob knew for a fact that it was exactly five meters long.

A quick search in the moonlight revealed nothing else of interest on the rooftop. Jacob crawled back through the door, closed it as quietly as he could, and switched on his flashlight. He followed an imaginary line down the stairs to the small table set to one side in the kitchen.

The light and soft sounds of the movement told him Jana was searching the floor just below. Jacob sat in the chair nearest the stairway to the roof and looked at the table. The oilcloth covering the table had four little depressions, each the size of a postage stamp in a rectangular pattern about the size of a toaster.

But there was a toaster on the counter to his right, next to the sink.

"Find anything?" Jana whispered from the stairwell.

"Yes. And you?"

"Something that doesn't fit." She started walking up the stairway. "In one of the bedrooms there's a stack of old tourist brochures to Tetouan, Tangier, Asilah, and bunch of attractions in the region. Plus a few business cards for local shops and taxi drivers. Then I found this."

She dropped a business card down in the center of the pattern Jacob was staring at. In the light of Jana's flashlight, he saw it was for a taxi driver in Karachi, in southern Pakistan. A bad cut-and-paste photo of a taxi was overlain on a green background, with the words "J. Khan Taxi Services" in English, along with a landline number and two mobile numbers. The card was creased, frayed a bit at the edges, and looked like it had been carried around for a long time.

"No other non-Moroccan stuff in that pile of brochures?" Jacob asked.

"Nope."

"Must have left in a hurry to leave behind evidence like that. Plus he should have shaken out this oilcloth, not that that would have fooled me. But at least I wouldn't be able to tell the dimensions of his radio."

"His radio?"

"The clothesline upstairs is made of copper wire, perfect for a radio antenna. It runs north-south, thus able to transmit a signal to the east and west, but he sloped it a bit so he could get a weaker signal to the north. There's a notch on the bottom of the door to feed a coaxial cable from the end of the antenna down to a radio he set up here."

"An end-fed long wire antenna," Jana said.

Jacob looked at her in surprise. Jana grinned.

"What? Did you think my dad didn't teach me about radios? How long is it?"

"Cut to five meters."

"Perfect for transmitting on a couple of amateur radio bands, or the frequencies between them."

Jacob nodded, looking around the kitchen in the hopes of finding more.

But while he and Jana would give the place a thorough search, he doubted they would find more than they already had—evidence of a compact transmitter and a hidden antenna. Proof that this had been a base from which to transmit intel.

This place had obviously been abandoned in a hurry, but a trained agent wouldn't slip up and leave any more evidence than what they had seen so far. He must have been in a hell of a hurry to slip up even this much.

All they had come up with was evidence that an agent for … someone … had been operating out of here. And that person had a connection to Karachi.

And that set off a memory in Jacob's mind.

They had been on R and R in London after yet another long mission. Aaron had taken them to an Indian restaurant for a curry because while both of them endured harsh deserts, long reconnaissance patrols, and brutal firefights, neither had the courage to face English food.

While at the restaurant, Jacob noticed the waiters weren't speaking Hindi, a language he couldn't speak but could recognize because of a couple of Indians he had worked with on an earlier mission.

"What language is that?" Jacob asked his mentor.

"Urdu," Aaron said, digging into his meal.

Urdu was the national language of Pakistan, and once or twice during their meal, Jacob noticed Aaron reacting to things the staff was saying to each other.

Aaron Peters knew how to speak Urdu. That wasn't a skill you just casually picked up. He had spent some time in-country. Over dinner that night, Jacob hadn't asked for details because Aaron wouldn't have been able to tell him anything, but it made sense. Pakistan was just over the Khyber Pass from Afghanistan, and Aaron had spent plenty of time on missions in Afghanistan. That's where the two of them had met. That's where Aaron had saved his soul.

A connection to Pakistan, a radio antenna aligned to broadcast in that direction. Had he been here?

Jacob ran his hand along the oilcloth, feeling each of the small divots left by the base of the transmitter.

Had he been here? Had Aaron Peters really been here, alive and still working? He had to find out, as much for his own peace of mind as Jana's.

CHAPTER FOUR

Jana knew she should really get some sleep, but the discovery earlier that night kept her mind running at a hundred miles an hour.

A connection to Pakistan, where Dad worked. A description of a fit Western man in his fifties living in an Airbnb that seemed to be a front for a mysterious, and perhaps fictitious, absentee landlord.

Jana tried not to get her hopes up. Jacob had told her everything about that final mission to Raqqa and how it looked like there was no chance that her father had made it out alive. She knew Jacob wouldn't have left without him if he thought there was a chance Dad had made it.

The radio could have been set up by anyone, and the taxi driver's business card from Pakistan proved nothing. That unstable country was a hotspot for espionage, terrorism, and drug running. Lots of agents for every spy agency worked in Pakistan.

They had found no real evidence that her father was alive. They hadn't even found any evidence that this Sydney Franke guy, someone Jana had never heard of, had stayed in the place. It could have been a different agent entirely.

Jana and Jacob sat in Jacob's hotel room in Tetouan's new city, far away from the medina and all its secrets. Hers was right next door. She sat on the edge of the bed while Jacob sat on a chair, both staring at the floor, each lost in their own thoughts. Neither had come up with a solution to the riddles they had found earlier that night.

Ghanem ibn Tariq had promised police surveillance on that house and the entire neighborhood, but they didn't hold out much hope for anything to come from that. Whoever had been there was long gone.

"When will your buddy get back to us?" Jana asked.

Jacob had a friend in an MI6 tracking station in Akrotiri looking into the phone numbers to see if they were linked to persons of interest.

"He's kind of busy right now. And it's not morning yet in Cyprus."

"What if it turns out to be just a regular taxi driver in Karachi?"

"Then we need to get someone in country to question him. I can arrange that."

“What if he doesn’t know anything? What if he drove Sydney or … my dad somewhere and doesn’t remember anything? What if he thought his ride was just another tourist or Western businessman?”

Jana could hear her voice rise, the tension coming out.

“Then we start over,” Jacob said. “We keep going until we get answers.”

“What if we never do? What if this is all pointless?”

Suddenly found herself crying. Crying for the father she lost, the bitterness of their relationship before she lost him, and all those wasted opportunities to make amends.

She felt ashamed of her tears, not because she was doing it in front of Jacob, who still irritated her as much as he helped her, but because it showed weakness in herself, and Dad had always raised her to be strong. Dad never cried.

Jana felt an arm go around her shoulders. She wiped her eyes and looked into Jacob’s.

“We’ll find out what really happened,” he told her. “I promise.”

“What if Raqqa really happened?” Jana asked, slumping.

“Then we prove it and get you closure.”

Jana sniffled. “If he’s dead, there’s no closure. I cut him off on my twenty-first birthday!”

After years of frequent, long, and unpredictable absences, Jana had given her father an ultimatum. She was about to graduate from university; that summer, she would be heading off on her first excavation in the Middle East, and her birthday was coming up. If he wasn’t there, their already rocky relationship would be over. Come to her birthday, that’s all she asked. He didn’t even have to bring her a gift. Just come. That commitment would be a gift enough.

But no. Work took him away. Again. He couldn’t say where he couldn’t say why, and he had no idea himself when he’d be back.

So he missed her birthday, and she stopped returning his calls.

And now he was probably dead, and some shadowy figure was using his personal code to communicate with Jacob.

Jacob gave her another squeeze. “He never stopped loving you. He always talked about you with me.”

Jealousy rose in her heart. In those last years, Dad had spent more time with Jacob than with her. She tried to suppress those negative feelings. He had been in a bad place, recovering from a serious breakdown, perhaps even a psychotic break, and he needed an older, more experienced agent to nurture him back to sanity.

But why did it have to be Dad? Why couldn't it have been someone else?

Because Dad was the best in the business, and now, thanks to Dad's training, Jacob is the best in the business.

"I'll do whatever it takes to find out the truth," Jacob said. "If I can make it right, I will."

Jana put her head on his shoulder, reassured by his protective manner. She had hated him for a long time for being this mysterious figure, a sort of ghost of a half-brother, who got to spend far more time with Dad than she did. She had barely known him back then, only briefly introduced a couple of times, and only later learned that most of the time Dad spent away had been spent with him.

That hatred had faded now that she understood what he had been through and how only Dad could have gotten him out of it. The hatred had faded into … what exactly?

Friendship? Sure, if getting into gunfights with terrorists and pirates constituted friendship. More? They had almost kissed on their last mission down in the Amazon, only to get interrupted when they thought their lives were in danger.

Jana breathed in his scent, nestled a little into the muscular shoulder. Well, they weren't in danger at the moment. But did she really want to take this step? It seemed like the world had thrown them together, so why fight it? Maybe have just a little …

… Jacob's satellite phone rang.

Damn it! This is worse than the Amazon. I didn't even have time to get started!

Jacob stood. Jana trailed her hand down his shoulder and bicep. He looked at her with interest. The satellite phone kept ringing. He made a face.

"Sorry."

And then he was hurrying off to the bathroom where he had hidden the phone in the cabinet under the sink, closing the door behind him.

***

Jacob answered the phone, even though he would have much rather filled up the bathtub and tossed the damn thing inside. The one time Jana wasn't griping at him and the phone had to ring! He could have sworn she was easing in for a kiss, like that time in camp down in the Amazon.

The voice of Station Director Tyler Wallace, his boss, came over the encrypted line.

"Hello, Agent Snow. How are you feeling? It's been a while since I spoke with you directly. I decided not to disturb you while you had some R and R."

"The injuries I sustained in the previous mission have all healed up, sir."

Jacob decided not to tell him about the grazing bullet wound in his side. It burned like hell, even though a medic from the Moroccan secret service had patched him up, reassuring him that the ribs hadn't been chipped. It sure felt like it, though.

"Good. I know you're on vacation—" at this point, Jacob had to pull his mouth away from the handset to keep his boss from hearing him laugh "—but we've got a critical situation in Pakistan."

"Pakistan!"

Suddenly Jacob was all ears.

"Yes, a couple of our agents, Robert Murphy and Oscar Dortmund, have been arrested by the provincial government of Balochistan and charged with spying."

"Oh hell, Robert and I came up together."

"I know. He's a good man."

"A damn good man."

"He and Agent Dortmund were pretending to be archaeologists in northwest Balochistan, near where its border meets with those of Afghanistan and Iran."

"What were they really doing?"

"Flying drones to look for Shia munitions dumps."

"Shia munitions dumps?" The Pakistani government was firmly Sunni. The two branches of Islam had been at each other's throats since the beginning of Islam. Iran and the area of Afghanistan, his boss mentioned, were majority Shia, as was a large minority population in Balochistan, but the government in Islamabad was firmly Sunni, as were the Gulf States that propped it up.

"Wait. Who arrested them again?"

"The regional government. There's a split going on in Balochi politics. The Shia minority is getting on top, and that makes the national government nervous. It could turn into civil war. I'm thinking the locals spied on them, figured out what they were up to, and nabbed them as a propaganda coup."

Jacob fell silent. The Pakistani government had long used nationalism and anti-Western feeling as part of its propaganda toolkit. If the local government of Balochistan could do that even better, they could demand concessions from Islamabad.

"So what's the provincial government doing now?" he asked at last.

"So far, all they've done is notify their superiors and the U.S. embassy."

"How did they react?"

"The embassy denied they were government employees and demanded their release. Islamabad demanded they be transferred to them. That hasn't happened. That won't happen."

Jacob shook his head. "They're not going to give up their bargaining chips. So what's next for getting them free?"

"On that front, what's next is up to the diplomats. I need you to do something a little more straightforward. Robert and Oscar's captors have not produced any evidence of spying. That means the agents were able to hide the data somewhere, probably at the site since that's where they were captured. I need you to go to Balochistan, locate it, and get it to our embassy in Islamabad."

"OK, but who's going to extract our agents?"

"We can't afford a mission for that. It's too likely to devolve into a gunfight, and that would ruin a very delicate diplomatic balance."

"Now wait a minute, we can't just hang them out to dry!"

"The diplomats are working on that."

"Who with? A bunch of politicians in Islamabad who aren't really in charge? The army that wants to go in guns blazing? A bunch of yokels in Balochistan who have no intention of giving them up?"

Wallace grunted, a bit irritated at his underling's tone, but only a bit. After saving the world a few times, Jacob had earned a good credit rating with the higher-ups.

"We have contacts in positions of influence."

"Please don't say the ISI. You know as well as I do they can't be relied on."

The Pakistani secret service called the Inter-Services Intelligence, didn't care about a pair of American archaeologists who they no doubt believed really were American spies. They were too busy quashing minority dissent and funding terror groups abroad. They had been instrumental in supporting the Taliban in the 1990s.

"That portion of our efforts doesn't concern you," Wallace said, sounding impatient. "I don't like it either, but the main priority is getting that data. Our satellite coverage can't compete with the close-ups that drone took. We need that detail. We need to know who is in what camp, which groups are in which hideouts."

"Oh."

Jacob nodded. That meant they were hunting someone specific. While spy satellites could see far, far more than the public realized, they had one serious problem—they saw everything from a bird's-eye view. The latest spy drones had excellent telescopic cameras, and by flying low, they could get long shots of people's faces and insignia.

"So who are these groups Robert and Oscar were spying on?"

"Three different ones. One is an ethnic Balochi ethnic militant group that's fighting inside Iran. They want the Balochi population along the border region to break off and unite with Pakistan."

"That's not going to happen."

"Tell them that. The other two groups are Shia militant groups fighting within Afghanistan. Both groups have a lot of Pakistani nationals in them and they occasionally come over the border to set off bombs in Pakistan."

"And the new Shia provincial government is supporting them?"

"We don't know the full extent of their support. That's one of the things we need the drone data for. Tracking individuals we know are linked to the Balochistan provincial government and seeing which groups they're working with and in what capacity. There's a lot more in a dossier I'll send you. All you want to know."

Jacob let out a derisive snort. The station director didn't even reply to that. They both knew that what the higher-ups decided Jacob Snow needed to know was far, far less than what he wanted to know.

Wallace went on. "You will take a cab to Tetouan Airport, where we have a plane waiting to take you to Islamabad. From there you'll have to make your way across country using whatever cover story you decide."

"That might take too long. Is this plane capable of flying low and slow enough for me to parachute out into Balochistan?"

"The pilot is Orhan Yildirim."

Jacob laughed. "Then he's capable of flying any plane as low and slow as he wants. He can make it dance the Macarena if you ask nice."

"Good luck to you, Agent Snow."

"Thank you, sir."

He hung up… and punched the wall. Their search for Aaron Peters had come to a dead end, and now he had to go save some data when he really should be saving two agents. The worst was that he had to shake Jana. No way she could come along on a mission like this, and of course, since it was Pakistan, she'd insist. She'd think it had something to do with that taxi driver's card they'd found. And it didn't. Did it?

CHAPTER FIVE

Jana had no intention of letting Jacob shake her. He'd done that too many times before.

Or tried to, anyway. Jana was beginning to think he enjoyed being followed and enjoyed being caught.

As soon as he had gone into that bathroom to answer his encrypted satellite phone, Jana knew they were sending him off on a mission.

She had stayed sitting on the bed for a moment, seething over the fact that the CIA was going to take Jacob from her just when she needed him the most.

But then her thoughts turned to the coincidence that they'd called just as the two of them were coming to a dead end in finding her father. This couldn't be related, could it?

Or could it?

So she had gotten up and tiptoed across the room.

Halfway to the bathroom door, she heard Jacob cry out, "Pakistan!"

Whoa, no way this is a coincidence.

She had hurried the last few remaining steps and pressed her ear to the door. While she only heard Jacob's half of the conversation, it told her enough.

Now she sat back in her place on the bed while Jacob hurriedly packed, telling her some story made up on the spot.

"They need backup for a European operation," he said, stuffing his clothes in an overnight bag. "It's a quick mission. Once I'm done in a few days, I'll call you and we can get back on track with this investigation."

I think you already are on track with this investigation, but you don't want to take me to Pakistan. That's a region for hairy-chested male CIA agents, right? Not female archaeologists.

She asked out loud: "How long do you estimate this mission will take?"

"I don't know. It's fairly straightforward, just getting in and performing an extraction. We have some planning to do that will take a couple of days."

You mean you have some traveling to do that will take a couple of days.

"I suppose it's out of the question that I go with you."

"CIA business. Sorry."

He finished his packing and, with his overnight back slung over one shoulder and another bag containing the satellite phone slung over the other, he paused for a moment, looking at her.

"What?" Jana asked, her heart beating a little faster.

He looked her in the eye. "I'm sorry I can't take you along. We work well together."

Then take me along.

Jacob took a step toward her. She raised her chin to look at him. He hesitated, gave a curt nod, and went out the door.

Oh, you're not getting away that easily!

Jana rushed to her room, packing in record time. Her dad had taught her to keep as much of her stuff packed when traveling as she could, so it made for a quicker getaway. She had learned that if one was traveling with Jacob Snow, that was twice as important.

It took her less than a minute, and she was out the door.

First stop was the hallway window, where she could peek out unseen through the wooden latticework at the street outside. It was one of the larger streets in the new portion of the city, and a taxi stand stood on the other side. Jacob was already heading across the street to it.

Jana rushed downstairs, past the front desk man whose question got cut off by the slamming of the hotel's front door, and Jana was out into the night.

She saw a taxi pulling away from the taxi stand. Cursing, Jana bolted across the road, causing a car to screech on its brakes, and made it to the taxi stand. Thankfully, another taxi was waiting there. She dove into the back seat and said, "Follow that taxi that just left."

The taxi driver looked in his rearview mirror. "I do not want trouble, madam."

Jana realized her sudden entrance and tone had made her look as suspicious as hell.

"Sorry, it's just that my husband is in the other cab."

He raised his eyebrows. "Husband?"

"I need to see where he's going. I mean, I think he might be … "

The taxi driver's eyes widened, then he flushed with embarrassment.

"I see, madam."

Without another word, he pulled away, merged with traffic, and tailed the other cab, which had only made it a block ahead.

This reminds me of Alexandria. I pulled the same stunt. That time it wasn't a cabbie but some poor schlep on his way to work. This guy drives better.

Indeed, the cabbie subtly wove in between other cars to close the distance, all the while keeping as out of sight as possible.

"Done this before?" Jana asked.

"Many bad husbands in Tetouan, madam."

They quickly passed out of town and into darker suburban streets that gradually gave way to farmland. Hills rose up all around, speckled with a scattered star map of village lights. Jana saw a sign for the airport.

Just as I thought.

Now that there were fewer cars on the road, the cabbie hung back, giving Jacob's cab some space.

The first cab got to the airport gate, the driver showed ID to the security guard and was waved through. By the time Jana's cab made it, the first cab was already well inside.

Tetouan's airport was a small one for private flights only, so it was pretty easy for Jana to spot which plane Jacob was going to. Unfortunately, that made it pretty easy for Jacob to spot that he was being followed.

As soon as he got out of his cab, he turned toward Jana's cab in the distance, looked right at it, and put his fists on his hips.

Uh-oh.

"You can pull up right here, I'll walk the rest of the way," she told the cabbie.

The cabbie stopped about twenty yards from her "husband."

"You will be all right, madam?"

"I'll be fine, thanks. Keep the change," Jana said, giving him far more than the fare. Her Moroccan dirhams wouldn't be worth anything where she was going, and knowing Jacob, she might not be coming back.

She got out. Jacob stood there, his face a mask, waiting for the cabs to leave. When they did so, he stormed forward. In the background, Jana could see the pilot standing next to a four-engine propeller plane, staring at them.

Jana walked toward him. Now that there were no innocent witnesses, Jacob opened up to her.

"What the hell do you think you're doing? You can't just ride along on a CIA mission. Sure, we needed you the first time as a consultant, and you kind of got swept up in the others, but this mission doesn't require your—"

His words cut off as Jana walked right by him, swinging her hand down as she passed to smack his butt.

A hard butt, she couldn't fail to notice, but that really came as no surprise.

Jana had made it almost to the plane before Jacob recovered. He ran after her, sputtering the words out.

"Hold on! You can't come!"

She ignored him, tossing her overnight bag into the open door of the plane. She saw it was an eight-seater private jet, probably with extra fuel tanks to make the long journey. She recognized the pilot as the same Turk who had flown them around Egypt several months before. He had a short, compact body, looked anywhere from his early thirties to late forties, and had a lean, wiry frame that emanated a sense of contained energy.

"What was your name again? Orhan something."

He made a mock bow. "Orhan Yildirim, at your service. Are you going to smack my butt too?"

"No."

"Too bad."

"She's not staying," Jacob said, coming up to them.

"I have contacts in Pakistan," Jana told him.

Jacob did a double take, then turned red. "You were listening in on a classified call?"

"I thought it was about … " she glanced at Orhan. " … what we were investigating."

"It isn't."

"You sure?"

Jacob's eyes got shifty. "Just because it's Pakistan doesn't mean it has to do with our, um, person of interest."

"He's more than a person of interest. I'm going."

Jacob reached in and grabbed her bag. "You're not."

"I am! I have every right to go."

Orhan chuckled. "You sound like my mother and father when they're fighting."

"Shut up," Jana and Jacob said in unison.

Jana grabbed her bag, tried and failed to pull it from the CIA agent's grasp, and glared at him.

"How were you planning on getting into Pakistan?" she asked.

"I was thinking of parachuting out near the area of interest." He looked beyond her to the pilot. "You can do that?"

"Not in this plane. I'm using this one for speed. But once we get to Dubai I'll switch to a Cessna Caravan. That one can fly under radar and slow enough for you to bail out. I have spare parachutes and can drop you within a five-meter radius."

"Good man."

"Good man, stupid idea," Jana said, giving her overnight bag another ineffective tug.

"And you got a better idea?"

"Use my contacts in country, like I said. I'm a member of the International Archaeological and Historical Heritage Fund. We raise money to help protect ancient sites threatened by urban expansion and natural erosion. There's a conference in Islamabad coming up next week. We can go using my accreditation."

"The Pakistanis aren't exactly happy with archaeologists right now."

"Why not?"

Jacob gave Orhan a significant look.

"Always a good idea to take a leak before a long flight," Orhan said. The pilot walked off toward the nearest hanger.

Jacob turned back to her. "We had two agents posing as archaeologists in Balochistan. The provincial government arrested them on charges of espionage."

"Was one of them Sydney or … "

"No."

"But the timing of that call is weird, you got to admit."

"Yeah."

"Wait, I was reading about the Balochistan elections last year. Didn't a coalition of Shia parties get in? The central government was trying to invalidate the elections, weren't they?"

"Yeah. But the provincial government held on. They're hoping for a big propaganda coup with this one."

"Well, then we won't have problems entering the country as archaeologists, as long as we land outside of Balochistan. The national government will want to show how reasonable they are, inviting scholars with open arms."

"Maybe." Jacob did not sound convinced.

"Think about it. The Balochistan government has set themselves at odds with the national government. So the Pakistanis will follow suit. The conference is still planned to happen. I didn't get any notice of a cancellation. And we call ourselves historians or architects, not archaeologists. Plenty of those go to the meetings."

"You can't come," Jacob said with less conviction than before.

Jana looked him in the eyes. "I have to come. Dad spent a lot of time in Pakistan. I figured that out from bits of conversation on the rare times he actually spent with me. If this has any connection to Dad, I need to be there."

"You know I'd share any information I got."

"That's not enough. I might notice something you don't. Plus I can help. I've been plenty of help on several missions now."

"It's dangerous."

"You think I don't know that? It doesn't *matter*, Jacob. I need to do this, and I don't need your permission."

Jacob rolled his eyes. "Meaning you'll go to Balochistan on your own, get into a bunch of trouble, and I'll have to bail you out and then be stuck with you."

"Condescending, but accurate enough."

"Jesus Christ. And there's no way to get you to see reason?"

"Nope!" she said with a smile.

Jacob tossed her overnight bag into the plane. "All right, get in. And don't make me regret this any more than I already do."

CHAPTER SIX

Jacob couldn't decide if he regretted caving in to Jana or not. He felt better having her along, safer even. Plus, having someone to talk to who didn't kill people for a living felt refreshing and kept his mind off all the filthy junk from his past that he dredged up far too often.

On the other hand, she was annoying as hell.

If his boss found out about this, he'd be eyebrows deep in meadow muffins. Being the best in the game earned him a good line of credit with the organization, but there were limits. He'd have to keep this quiet.

He didn't have to worry about Orhan. The Turkish-American was a mercenary, selling his services to the highest bidder but keeping in the good graces of the CIA by only hiring out to national security organizations. Of course, some of those nations were hostile to the West, but he never dealt with drug runners, human traffickers, or terrorists. If those people approached him, he handed over their details.

For money, of course. Jacob couldn't blame him for that. A man had to earn a living.

But he'd never sell Jacob's information, and he wouldn't try to blackmail him. Good and evil came on a spectrum, and Orhan Yildirim was comfortably on the good side. Not too far from the center, but far enough.

No, what he had to worry about was any operatives in the country spotting her with him or trouble from the provincial government.

Outside his window, he saw the black expanse of the eastern Mediterranean, with only a couple of lights from freighters or container ships shining far below. The hum of the engines lulled him. He should get some sleep.

But he couldn't help thinking of poor Robert. When he joined the CIA, Robert was a fresh young agent with only a few years of experience. Although Jacob was brand new to the organization, he had Ranger training and combat experience, while Robert had come from a university with an honors degree in International Studies and a talent for languages that was truly amazing.

On their first mission together, they had gone down to Chiapas to do some surveillance work, and within two weeks, Robert was having conversations in Chiapanecan Mayan. Jacob couldn't even pronounce the word for the language, which was something like "Tojol-ab'al."

Over the course of that trip, Robert and Jacob sized each other up, decided they were about even, and became fast friends. Robert taught Jacob some tricks of the trade, and Jacob helped Robert with his hand-to-hand combat skills.

He didn't know anything about Oscar Dortmund other than he had worked with Robert on several missions, so he must be good. He was worth saving too.

It killed him to think he was only being sent to retrieve some lousy data and leave Robert and Oscar to fester in the hellhole of a prison the locals had put them in. He wasn't sure what he could do about it, however.

Since he knew sleep wouldn't come for a while, he flipped through the briefing again. Jana sat in a seat nearby, watching him and no doubt hoping to be invited to peek over his shoulder.

He ignored her. He'd given away too much classified information already.

Of the three groups the provincial government was funding, the Iranian dissident group was the only new one to him. There wasn't much intel on it except that it appeared to have emerged only in the past year, just when the elections put the Shia into power in Balochistan.

But that didn't make sense. Iran was the powerbroker for the Shia religion. Why go against them? Something else was going on there.

The next group was more familiar. The Hazara Liberation Front was based in the Hazara ethnic community, which was mostly Shia. Their traditional lands straddled the border of Afghanistan and Pakistan's Balochistan province. The group didn't need funding, making good money from smuggling and local taxes in their area of control, but the provision of safe camps on the Balochi side of the border must have come as a nice bonus.

The third group made Jacob wince. The Sons of Imam Ali was one of the nastier terrorist groups out there. Funded by Iran and now funded by this new provincial government, they had set themselves up as defenders of the minority Shia faith in Afghanistan.

There was a lot to defend. The Taliban persecuted the Shia, and the local branch of the Islamic State killed them whenever they got the chance. So the Sons of Imam Ali went after both. Their favorite method of execution was to pour boiling water over their captives.

Usually, the CIA worked on the old principle of "the enemy of my enemy is my friend," but not after the group killed fifteen aid workers, several of them from the U.S. and allied nations.

That got them on the hit list, and the job went to Jacob.

He had gone in the previous year and captured their leader so he could bring him to a CIA black site where he could be interrogated. Unfortunately, he got spotted while withdrawing, and now he was on their hit list.

And if they were getting funding and support from the provincial government of Balochistan, things could get very messy for him.

After all, the friend of my enemy is my enemy, especially the way these guys play.

Jacob put away the folder and shut his eyes. Despite his worries over his fellow agents, and the danger he was in going into what he now knew was enemy territory, he fell asleep within two minutes.

It was a trick he had learned in the Rangers. The best way to deal with future danger wasn't to worry about it but to prepare for it by getting as much rest as possible. Only then would you be in top shape to face whatever challenges came at you.

Except with that burning wound in his side and a civilian tagging along, he would be anything but in top shape.

***

Robert Murphy sat in a ten-foot by ten-foot windowless cell. A musty old army sleeping bag in the corner passed for a bed. In the other corner was a festering hole in the floor that served as a toilet. Robert sat next to the door, where a peephole and a slit to pass food through were the only sources of fresh air.

Unfortunately, being positioned close to the door meant he could hear Nadeem's screams more clearly.

They had been torturing the graduate student for a couple of hours now in a chamber filled with devices expertly designed to cause pain. He had seen it when the police had taken them to the cells. To get to the cells, you had to pass right through the torture chamber. The architect was smart when he designed the floor plan. Maybe the bastard had a dual degree in psychology.

"I know nothing!" Nadeem screamed for the hundredth time, followed by a shriek of pain.

Robert gritted his teeth and saved his breath. He had told them again, and again the foreman was innocent, but since Robert was still proclaiming his own innocence, they didn't believe him. And admitting he was a spy would only make them redouble their efforts to extract a confession from the foreman.

Robert peeked out of the slit where they shoved his food through. It was at the bottom of the door, and he had to get on his hands and knees to do it. He had already brushed the dead cockroaches away from that spot so they wouldn't get in his hair.

His view was limited to a stretch of hallway about a yard long. Opposite him was a blank wall; the doors were staggered so no prisoner would have direct contact with any other.

"Oscar, you here?" he whispered.

He had heard the guards dragging someone into one of the nearby cells. He hadn't looked when they passed. The last time he looked, they jabbed a truncheon through the slit and gave him a black eye.

No reply. He and Oscar had been separated at the military base where the soldiers had taken them. He hadn't seen him since.

He switched to Urdu.

"Who is that in the next cell?"

A groan was the only reply.

"Can you hear me? Who is that?"

"Mind your own business, unbeliever. I'm in enough trouble. I won't speak to spies."

Robert remained crouched where he was for a moment. It was cold and uncomfortable, but at least this little stretch of hallway was something new to look at. The walls of his cell were blank except for a few bloodstains.

The screams from the torture chamber had stopped. It was only about ten yards down the hall, and in the echoing concrete underground where he had found himself, Robert could hear all the details—the straps being unbound, someone's heavy breathing, the thud of his body hitting the floor, but no groan. Was he unconscious or dead?

Then he heard booted footsteps and the sliding sound of a man's body being dragged on the floor. He moved away from the feeding slit so he didn't get another black eye.

The body was dragged past, the guards breathing heavily. He heard the body thump as they dropped him, the door clang shut, the bolt slammed into position, and the boots walked back. There sounded like there were three or four of them.

They stopped in front of his cell door. Robert took a deep breath and prepared himself.

A rapping sound. It took a moment for him to realize what it was.

Knocking. They were knocking on his door. Mocking him.

"Anybody home?" asked the colonel's voice in English. "May we come in?"

The other soldiers laughed. They probably didn't speak English—they were just sucking up to their officer.

"Nadeem is an innocent man," Robert said. "Leave him alone. He's loyal to the government."

"Oh, so he didn't know you were spying?"

"We weren't spying."

"We have found irrefutable evidence!" the colonel shouted.

Robert doubted that was true. If it was, the colonel would have told him about finding the thumb drive hidden in the excavation square.

He hoped whoever came to extract the intel would figure out where he hid it. Robert was betting on them sending Jacob Snow. The CIA field office in Islamabad would hesitate to send any of the agents they had in the country. There had been a recent breach of security, and they feared many of the agents had been compromised, although they weren't sure who. That's why they sent Robert and Oscar in the first place. They'd been working in Latin America for the last couple of years and weren't known locally.

They sure were now. The soldiers had taken their photos before they smacked them around. Their faces were probably on every newspaper and website in the country.

Jacob hadn't been to Pakistan recently either, as far as he knew, although he had plenty of experience in Afghanistan. So yeah, if Jacob was available, they'd probably send him. He was the best agent the CIA had who wasn't potentially compromised in Pakistan.

Robert just had to hope that Jacob would figure out the clues he left as to the hiding place; otherwise, he might never find the thumb drive, and then his suffering, Oscar's suffering, and poor Nadeem's suffering would be in vain.

A fist hit the metal door of his cell, making him jump.

"We are going to have some tea now, spy. Once we are done, we will come for you, and we will show you more pain than that filthy traitor we just finished with."

CHAPTER SEVEN

Jana rubbed her eyes and stepped out of Orhan's Cessna. She had grabbed a few hours of sleep on the plane and now looked out at the ugly tarmac and concrete hangers of Karachi's Jinnah International Airport.

She hoped those few hours of sleep would last her because she got the feeling she wouldn't be getting much for a while.

They had landed in the section for smaller, private planes, which was too bad. In a country like this, that section always had tighter security than the one for big commercial flights.

Jana readied herself, bade goodbye to Orhan, who she had a funny feeling she'd be seeing again, and walked across the tarmac with a yawning and sleepy-eyed Jacob. The air was loud with the sound of jet engines and smelled of a mixture of pollution and the salty tang from a hot wind blowing in off the Arabian Sea. A pair of vigilant soldiers toting machine guns flanked the entrance to a building that had a sign saying "Customs and Security" in Urdu, English, and Arabic.

They passed through, placed their bags on the conveyor belt to the x-ray and went through a metal detector, all under the watchful gaze of more soldiers.

While she hadn't been to Karachi for a few years, there seemed to be a lot more security now, and they acted a lot more suspiciously. The situation with the two alleged spies, whose story was headline news all over the world now, had gotten them keyed up.

On a brief stop in Dubai to change planes, they had checked their phones and found grim-faced photos of Roger Murphy and Oscar Dortmund on every news site. Jacob had also managed to get in touch with his British contact in Cyprus, only to find that the numbers on the business card they had found in the Tetouan safehouse weren't Pakistani phone numbers at all or phone numbers for anywhere else. Yet another thing on their long list of mysteries to figure out.

The first challenge, though, was getting through customs, a row of bulletproof booths just past the security check.

This early in the morning, there was barely a line. Jana took a couple of minutes to get to the front to take on the calm, somewhat bored expression she always used with customs officials. Nothing to see here. Just another jetlagged foreigner passing through.

"Let me take the lead on this," Jana murmured.

"A woman is always more disarming," Jacob whispered back.

Sexist, but true enough. No one ever suspects a woman of international espionage.

It came their turn, and they stepped up to the window, behind which a heavyset man with beady eyes studied them with a mixture of weariness and suspicion. They handed over their passports.

"Purpose of visit?" he asked in English.

"We're attending the meeting of the International Archaeological and Historical Heritage Fund in Islamabad next week," Jana said.

Those beady eyes fixed on her.

"Why did you fly to Karachi then, and on a private plane?"

Damn good questions, but Jana had anticipated them.

"I was attending a party in Dubai hosted by the Sheik Mohammed ibn Harun. He arranged for a private flight. He's a good friend."

Or wanted to be. The Sheik Mohammed ibn Harun was sixty years old, bald as a tea kettle, and had a belly big enough that, if hollow, Jana could have comfortably curled up inside. Despite these failings, he was enamored with archaeology and donated lavishly to digs all across the Middle East, including Jana's own. He was enamored with her as much as with archaeology, although he kept his hands, if not his eyes, to himself.

If the customs official plucked up the courage to call the sheik, Mohammed ibn Harun would back up any story Jana gave.

The customs official gave her a knowing look, assuming that the sheik's dreams had become a reality. Then he looked at Jacob.

"And who are you?"

"Professor Lewis Hanson," Jacob said, giving the name that was on his passport. "I study history."

The customs official looked back and forth between the foreign man and the foreign woman. "So you are married?"

"Colleagues," Jana said.

Again that knowing twinkle in those beady eyes. The twinkle soon vanished, replaced with the usual suspicion.

"Why fly to Karachi?"

He asked Jacob, the man, but it was Jana who answered. "Because we wanted to see some of the great historic monuments of your city—

the Mohatta Palace and the Chaukandi Tombs. And of course the great Shah Jahan mosque. Then we'll take a train north to Islamabad."

The customs official's face hardened with annoyance, and he continued to speak with Jacob.

"Which of these places do you like the most?"

"Oh, I haven't been here before. My colleague says all of them are worth seeing. I'm more of a specialist in Pre-Columbian art and architecture, especially the civilization centered around Teotihuacan."

More like you're a specialist in getting into gunfights and disabling bioweapons over there, Jana thought, trying to keep from smiling.

"You are?" the customs official said.

"Certainly! The Late Preclassic Mayan monumental buildings are most impressive, don't you think? And I'm sure you'd agree that there's a clear tie with Toltec architecture, especially that found in Panama."

Total babble, but this guy doesn't know that.

"I think you will find the monuments in Pakistan to be even more impressive."

The customs official stamped their passports and let them through.

"Don't try that line in an academic conference," Jana whispered once they were through the customs area.

"We aren't going to an academic conference, we're going to the bad side of town."

"Do you ever go to the good side of town?"

"Nah, too boring."

"And why are we going to the bad side of Karachi?"

"There's a salesman there who has a few things we're going to pick up."

Jana rolled her eyes. That sounded like trouble.

***

Jacob peered out the taxi window as the driver took them to the eastern outskirts. Just a few minutes before, an operative had met them a mile down the road from the airport to hand Jacob a laptop with a satellite phone hookup, along with a compact shortwave transceiver with a loop of copper wire as an antenna. Other than a curious look at Jana, he had said nothing and left without a word.

After that, they took a second taxi and soon had left the small, modern downtown area of skyscrapers far behind, as well as the more historical areas that probably contained those monuments Jana had mentioned to the customs official.

He had never seen them. He'd passed through Karachi a few times, but he had never had to opportunity to play the tourist. It would be nice to stroll through some historical sites with someone who knew about and appreciated all that stuff, but they didn't have the time on this visit either.

Now the taxi took them along a highway on the outskirts of town, past warehouses and sites for light industry, the sea breeze not quite clearing the haze that hung above the area, a combination of smog and dust. Behind the row of industrial buildings, Jacob could catch glimpses of long streets flanked by ugly concrete homes and apartment buildings, residences for the poorer civilians of this booming port city. While a bit run down, it did not appear menacing.

"I thought this was the bad part of town," Jana said, peering out the window too. She wore a loose pair of cotton slacks, an even looser shirt buttoned up to the neck, and a bright yellow headscarf. While she was still obviously a Western woman, respecting local sensitivities was always a good idea.

"Appearances can be deceiving."

Jana nudged him. "Like you appearing to be a tough, no-nonsense modern-day Rambo?"

"What's that supposed to mean?"

"You didn't even try to ditch me in a hotel."

"We don't have time to go to a hotel. Besides, you wouldn't have stayed there. If I have to take care of you, it's better to have you in sight."

"I thought I was taking care of you."

"Get real."

Jana smiled and nudged him again.

"You think you don't need someone to take care of you? You're a walking disaster."

"Har har."

He wished she'd cut the sarcasm and slap his butt again. That was nice and surprising. Not culturally appropriate in Pakistan, however. Although now that they were past customs and in the country, they'd have to pose as man and wife. Unlike in more relaxed Morocco, in Pakistan, unmarried men and women couldn't stay in the same hotel room, not even foreigners, and for safety's sake, they had to stay in the same hotel room.

The thought of it gave Jacob all sorts of feelings, a mixture between interest, trepidation, and depression. There was some chemistry going on between them, something budding feeling that he knew couldn't really come to fruition while they were on a mission.

And he wasn't sure he wanted it to come to fruition. He was still in mourning over Gabriella, his on-again, off-again girlfriend who got killed in a hit intended for him.

Getting close to him was a dangerous thing for a woman. And he didn't think he was ready for anything anyway. There had barely been room in his life for someone like Gabriella, who had been just as devoted to her career as he was and wanted to see him whenever it was convenient, no strings attached?

Jana wasn't that sort of person. She went 110% into whatever she did, and Jacob suspected relationships were no exception.

Keep your fantasies under control, buddy. They aren't going to turn into reality.

Besides, we're just about there, and once we get what we need and get on the road, you're going to need all of your concentration to make it through the next few days alive.

CHAPTER EIGHT

"Mark, my good friend!"

Hashir Khan stood in front of his mechanic's shop, clad in grubby overalls spattered with grease. His hands, outstretched in greeting, were black from fixing engines, and the smile that parted his beard dyed red with henna did not reach his eyes.

Jacob clasped him about the shoulders and exchanged a kiss on each cheek as if Hashir Khan was a friend, which he was not. Hashir was a businessman, nothing more, and an untrustworthy one at that.

Jacob, known as Mark to this career criminal, clasped him in a friendly hug. After a moment, Hashir looked over his shoulder at Jana.

"I see you have found yourself a wife."

"Um, yeah," Jacob said, unsure if Hashir believed his own words.

"Come, let me show you what I have for you."

They passed into the garage, where an old Nissan, a battered Land Rover, and a truck were all lined up. The hood to the truck was up, and a boy of about eleven in stained overalls, standing on a box so he could reach, was adjusting something with a socket wrench.

"Hey, Mark!" the kid said in English.

"Still working for this scumbag, Mohammed?" Jacob replied.

"You can't pick your family like you pick your friends," Mohammed replied, parroting a line Jacob had taught him the last time he was here.

"Bah! You make a son disrespect his father," Hashir said without anger.

"That's because you're disrespectable."

"Makes good money, though," Mohammed chimed in. "We just built an extension to the house and he bought me a Playstation 5."

"Good. You deserve it."

"You won't deserve it if you don't finish tuning that truck," Hashir said. Then he turned to Jacob. "How can I help you today, my friend?"

"I need the full package."

His eyebrows went up. His eyes gleamed with greed. "The full package?"

"The works. What do you got?"

Hashir smiled and extended a hand toward the Land Rover.

"The finest transportation money can buy!"

"It looks like it's been through the Khyber Pass a hundred times and got ambushed every time."

"Nonsense, my friend. Open the door."

Jacob did so and found it heavier than usual. "You put armor plating inside?"

"On every spot. It will stop small arms rounds. The engine has been gone over and the suspension strengthened by myself and Aalim."

Jacob looked around for Hashir's capable assistant. "Where is he, anyway?"

"He, um, is taking a vacation."

"In prison," Mohammed added, not looking up from his work.

"Keep your mouth shut or no video games!" his father shouted.

Mohammed giggled.

"The Land Rover has everything, my friend. GPS, spare fuel tank, a full toolkit, everything."

"We'll have to take it for a test drive," Jana said.

Hashir gave her an irritated look as if she was interrupting the conversation and continued to address Jacob.

"When you say you need everything, does that mean you need to see the basement?"

"Your tomb of treasures? You bet I do."

Hashir gave Jana a suspicious look.

"She's with me," Jacob said.

Hashir shrugged and headed to the back of the garage. They followed him past an engine block sitting on a palette and through a narrow hall to a storage room. Hashir pushed aside a box of windshield wipers to reveal what looked like just another part of the concrete floor. He pressed an oil stain on the floor, and there was a loud click, followed by an electric hum. A rectangle in the floor opened up. Jacob could not help but notice it was the same size and dimensions as a grave.

A wooden stairway led down to a dimly lit cellar. Hashir led them down the steps, everyone having to bow their heads, and they ended up in a large underground room almost as big as the building above them.

Jana let out a low whistle. The walls were lined with gun racks containing firearms of all descriptions—assault rifles, sniper rifles, shotguns, and submachine guns. Several shelves held pistols, and at the far end stood another rack of rocket-propelled grenade launchers. In the center of the room were several mortars, heavy machine guns on tripods, and crates of grenades and ammunition.

"How's your budget?" Hashir asked.

"Juicy."

The arms dealer smiled. "It always is with you, my friend."

And that's why you call me friend.

Jacob paced through the room, feeling like that kid in the proverbial candy shop.

The easy picks first—he grabbed half a dozen fragmentation, smoke, and stun grenades. Then he moved over to the gun rack, where Jana was trying out a PK-21 assault rifle, the most common model in these parts because it was army issue. Not the best choice technically speaking, but the best tactically speaking. If they got in a fight with the authorities, her shots would sound the same as theirs.

Hashir watched as Jana checked the magazine, racked the bolt, and sniffed the barrel.

"All my guns are new, except for the bargain bin over there," Hashir said, indicating to a rack on the other side of the cellar filled with an array of beat-up old rifles and AK-47s that looked like refugees from one of Afghanistan's endless wars.

Jacob scanned the rack of better armaments, and after mulling over the possibilities, grabbed a PK-21 himself, inspected it, and then added an attachable GP-34 grenade launcher.

Next, he picked up a PSR-90 sniper's rifle used by the Special Service Group in the Pakistani military. It was a hell of a rifle, with an effective range of 1000 yards and deadly accurate at 300. It was also semiautomatic, which was a nice bonus. He'd never used one in the field, however, so after fondling it for a minute, he put it away and instead chose an Austrian-made Steyr SSG 69, a bit less accurate and with an effective range of 200 yards less than the Pakistani model. This older sniper's rifle was still a good weapon, however, and more importantly, he had a lot of experience with it. Hashir had also fitted it with an excellent scope.

"You fire test this scope for accuracy?" Jacob asked.

"I test all my guns before sale, my friend."

That was probably true, but Jacob would feel a lot better once he stopped in some lonely stretch of desert and fire-tested it himself. You never relied on anyone else to take care of your weapons if at all possible.

Next-they each grabbed a pair of Beretta 92 9mm pistols, once again because they were standard army issue and their sounds would meld into the enemies on the battlefield.

Now that he thought of it, Jacob realized that pretty much everything here was Pakistan army issue. That made him wonder how Hashir got his product.

Probably from some corrupt quartermaster, but Jacob knew better than to ask. He'd never get an answer.

"You got any zip cuffs?"

"For tying hands? Certainly, my friend. In that box over there."

After loading up on zip cuffs, plenty of ammunition, and throwing a pair of walkie talkies in for good measure, Jacob nodded to the arms dealer.

"This should just about do it. Looks like you can treat little Mohammed to some extra video games."

"Bah! He plays them too much. Today boys are lazy. Why did Allah only give me one son and five daughters?"

"Probably to punish you for the bill you're about to give me."

Hashir grinned. "Oh yes, the bill."

The amount it came to was extortionate, but Orhan had handed him a hefty wad of $100 bills courtesy of the CIA, so Jacob counted out the amount. It took some time.

"A pleasure doing business as always, Hashir."

"Do you need a guide?"

"Nope."

"Travel advice?"

"Sure." Jacob handed him an extra $500. Hashir's travel advice was usually worth it.

"Where are you going?"

"Balochistan Province."

Hashir's eyebrows went up. He rubbed his hennaed beard for a moment.

"To Zaranka?"

Hashir knew Jacob was CIA. Not that he had ever told him, but Hashir was as intelligent as he was corrupt.

"Maybe."

"A tricky place, my friend. There is trouble, and not just the trouble with the hostages."

"What other trouble is there?"

"With this new Shia government in power, the Sunnis have gotten angry. They have created militias to attack isolated vehicles and Shia villages. The police and army try to stop them, but as you know the province is big, with many empty places to hide. Travel in those areas is very dangerous."

"We'll be careful. We don't want to be caught up in any religious feuding."

Hashir shook his head. "It's not a religious fight, my friend. Not really. The Sunni bandits are using that as an excuse, because there are Sunni villages, rivals to the Shia ones, who shelter them and give them food and gasoline. The central government should get rid of that new government in Balochistan. It causes nothing but trouble."

They gathered up the armaments and walked up the stairs to the main floor. Jacob wondered how much Hashir hated the new Balochi government for causing instability in a country already teetering on the edge and how much he hated it because it was Shia and he was Sunni. Just because he was a criminal didn't mean he lacked deeply held views on religion. A lot of people in the Middle East's underworld would kill a man for a hundred dollars but wouldn't insult the Prophet for a million.

As they got to the storeroom, Jacob could see the light in the hallway had dimmed. There was no more daylight filtering in. Mohammed had shut the garage door. Good kid. Jacob wondered if the next generation of CIA agents would be buying weapons from him or if he'd go a different path from his father.

As much as the first option amused him, it depressed him too.

When they got to the garage, they found the boy filling up the Land Rover from a jerry can.

"Hey, Mohammed, your dad just made a bundle of money."

The boy grinned, showing uneven teeth. "He's great at that."

Jacob stretched out an arm. "One day, all this will be yours."

Mohammed nodded, focusing on filling the tank.

"What do you want to be when you grow up?"

"An arms dealer. What else?"

Jacob shrugged. "Anything else."

"What do you mean?"

"You're going to inherit money and land. You could set yourself up in any business."

"It's written that I'll be an arms dealer like my father. Just like it's written that you're a CIA assassin."

Jacob felt like he'd just been punched in the stomach by a prizefighter.

Mektoub. "It is written." God had decided everyone's fate, and no one could change it.

Mohammed was fated to follow in his father's footsteps, and Jacob was fated to do what he did.

An assassin. That's what the kid thinks I am, Jacob thought as he stowed the weapons in a secret compartment, he showed him beneath the seats. *Does he have me wrong, or does he see me better than I see myself?*

CHAPTER NINE

Jana looked out the window of the Land Rover as they sped along a dusty highway in Balochistan. They had been driving for hours, successfully passing through police roadblocks on the outskirts of Karachi and then at regular intervals along the way. Hashir's secret compartments were masterpieces of obfuscation.

They made good time, Jacob going eighty and weaving past slower cars and the big lumbering trucks one found everywhere in Pakistan. They were giant things, painted in complex patterns of gaudy colors, with metal medallions dangling from their fenders to catch the light and make a tinkling sound as they passed. They'd have been beautiful except for the exhaust they belched from their poorly tuned engines running on cheap fuel.

As they drove north and west, passing over the provincial border and into Balochistan, the farmland of the coast quickly gave way to rocky desert hills with only a few patches of scrub and long, flat stretches of gritty desert, its surface blinding from the harsh sun.

Occasionally they passed a village or town—dusty, impoverished places that survived off of herding, a bit of meager farming thanks to deep wells, and selling gasoline and food to passing motorists.

In a few spots, she saw what could only be called truck stops. Several of the big, colorful rigs would be parked outside a large café covered with an awning, the men reclining on wood frame benches covered with a latticework of rope called *charpai*, sipping tea and talking.

She saw virtually no women. There were none in the cafes, none in the shops. Occasionally she'd one on the back of a motorcycle driven by a man or in the passenger's seat of a passing car. Sometimes she'd see mothers and girls doing the shopping in the village markets. Most wore the burka, or a strange variation worn by the Balochi tribeswomen, the face covered by a rigid cloth mask of colored strips, with a central ridge running from the nose to the mouth that made them look like birds with colorful faces. The only skin they showed was their hands and sandaled feet.

Jana realized that if it wasn't for the tinted windows of the Land Rover, she'd stick out like a sore thumb. The soldiers at the checkpoints had certainly stared, and Jacob had to reassure them that she was his wife.

She wondered if he resented her coming, resented her complicating the mission. He hadn't said anything for miles.

She struggled for something to say.

Jana let out a little chuckle. "Hashir and Mohammed remind me of Néstor and Eva."

"They're nothing like Néstor and Eva," Jacob grumbled.

Jana bit her lip. He was right, of course. The father-daughter smuggling team down in the Caribbean didn't run guns. While they didn't exactly live within the law, they didn't have blood on their hands.

They lapsed into silence again. Jacob had left the highway and drove along a gravel road past increasingly rare villages before the road turned into nothing but a track running along the dirt floor of a long valley running between rows of sun-blasted stone hills to either side. Other than the wheel marks and a distant plume of dust far ahead that must have been from a truck, there wasn't a sign of humanity.

Jacob gave her a couple of sidelong glances, licked his lips, and said, "Sure is bleak out here. I wonder if Robert and Oscar found anything. Maybe that's why their cover was blown. The Balochis couldn't believe they would actually dig out here."

Jana could see he was trying to make conversation, so she played along.

"This is one of the richest archaeological regions in the world."

"I'm afraid I'm not up on the archaeology of Pakistan," Jacob said.

"Oh, there's an incredible amount here. One of the earliest Neolithic sites in the world is in Balochistan, not far from that village where we're going. It's called Mehrgarh and there's evidence of farming as early as nine thousand years ago. It wasn't just a farming village either. They made elaborate figurines and jewelry and traded for lapis lazuli as far away as northeastern Afghanistan, over the mountains and hundreds of miles away."

"What's lapis lazuli?"

"It's a blue semiprecious stone. You know the blue decoration on the mask of King Tutankhamun? That's lapis lazuli."

"Did the Egyptians get it from Afghanistan too?"

"Yeah. It's the only source in the Old World other than Angola."

"That's a long way to travel for some pretty stones."

"The ancients had extensive trade networks. A lot of people think ancient people were stuck in their villages doing simple farming, and while that was true for the bulk of the population, others sailed the seas or traveled in caravans across continents."

"Huh. Isn't the Indus Valley civilization in Pakistan too?"

"That started later, a little before five thousand years ago at the beginning of the Bronze Age. It had large urban centers and spread over a huge area, even more than Ancient Egypt and the Mesopotamian city-states."

"Huh. Interesting."

Jana could see Jacob's eyes begin to glaze over. While he did show some interest in ancient civilizations, his interest would quickly flag if she started to get technical.

"Maybe we'll have a chance for some sightseeing once this is all done," she suggested.

Jacob snickered. "Yeah, that always happens on missions."

Jana smiled. "Oh, come now. We've seen a lot. Usually while running from bad guys and getting shot at, but I try to take it all in."

Jacob nodded, fell silent for a minute, then said softly, "It would be nice to actually go on a trip where I didn't have to shoot at people."

Jana remembered his expression when little Mohammed had called him an assassin.

She reached over, hesitated, then put her hand on his shoulder.

"You have a dirty job, Jacob, I'm not going to lie, but you do what you have to do. Once you explained to me what you called the 'mathematics of power' or something like that. If you act, a bunch of people will die. If you don't act, a bunch more people will die. You do the math and come up with your answer."

Jacob mumbled something incomprehensible. She thought she caught the phrase "collateral damage."

She paused, struggling for the right thing to say.

"Yes, innocent people get hurt … " she cut off when he gave her a sharp look, then rallied " … they sometimes get killed, but if you let the bad guys get away with it, even more people will get killed. You're a force for good in the world, Jacob."

"Whatever."

"You are," she insisted.

You have to be. Because if you're not, what am I?

He sat hunched over, staring straight ahead, knuckles white on the wheel. Far ahead, the truck turned off on a side track and made for the mountains to their right. Headed … somewhere. Jacob was right—there seemed to be nothing in this bleak landscape.

In the rearview mirror, she saw some more plumes of dust kicked up by vehicles far behind them. At least they wouldn't be entirely alone.

Not like Jacob.

She had let her hand fall. She put it on his shoulder again and squeezed.

"Look what we're doing right now. We're retrieving that intel, and then we're going on a rescue mission for your buddies."

"Right." Jacob growled. "A rescue mission for my buddies."

Jana wondered why he was acting so glum. It didn't look like he was going to talk, though. Hanging out with him was like hanging out with a Greek statue. Magnificent body, but cold and silent.

She let her hand fall again and stared out the window at the empty landscape.

"Uh-oh," Jacob said after a minute.

He was looking in the rearview mirror. Those dust plumes had gained on them and had resolved into four Jeeps, coming up fast.

"What was that Hashir said about bandits?" Jana asked.

"Yeah," Jacob said, putting on some speed and keeping an eye on the rearview mirror. "Yeah, I think you should bust out the weapons."

Jana bent over, flipped a hidden catch, and opened up the secret compartment under her feet. She pulled out both assault rifles, including Jacob's with the grenade launcher, as well as the grenades. She also pulled out the pistols, just in case things got too intimate.

Of course, this could just be a caravan of Jeeps in a hurry somewhere, but in this region, and riding with someone like Jacob Snow, it paid to be careful.

"We're switching places," Jacob said.

"Why?"

"Because I'm the better shot."

That was true, but it wasn't the reason for the deep sense of relief she felt at this command. She hated killing, had done way too much of it since Jacob came into her life, and she wanted to avoid it as much as she could.

Jana lifted herself up, Jacob squeezed beneath her, and for an awkward moment, Jana found herself sitting in his lap.

Then she was in the driver's seat and hitting the accelerator. In the brief moment, no one's foot was on the gas—the Jeeps had gained on them. A lot.

Even worse, they had spread out. Only one drove on the track now, the others having taken up positions to either side.

Jacob rolled down the window. Jana put her 9mm automatic pistol in her lap and rolled down hers. Hot wind and grit hit her face. It was a good thing she had on shades, or the grit would have blinded her in an instant.

"Don't shoot unless they shoot at us first," Jana said.

"I'm not a damn psycho," Jacob growled.

"You're not an assassin either," Jana replied, remembering Mohammed's offhand yet hurtful comment.

"I will be if these assholes try anything."

The Jeeps drew closer. Jana could make out two men in each cab and several more in each bed. So far, no sign of weapons.

Those came out pretty quick when they got close enough.

All of a sudden, at some hidden signal, the men in the backs of the Jeeps rose up, each wielding a Kalashnikov. The men in the passenger's sides of the cabs leaned out the window, doing the same. A couple fired rounds to either side of Jana and Jacob's Land Rover, kicking up dirt. Warning shots. Stop or die.

Yeah, right. If they stopped, they'd die—Jana much later than Jacob. They'd make her suffer first.

Jana hit the brakes and swerved to the left. The sudden move caught the bandits by surprise, and before they knew it, Jana was beside them, driving at the same speed at the end of their line. Now only one Jeep could fire at them instead of all four. And that's when Jacob Snow unleashed hell.

CHAPTER TEN

Jacob braced his legs on the inside of the Land Rover's door. That crazy driving Jana just pulled had nearly thrown him out of the damn vehicle.

The guys in the nearest Jeep looked a bit stunned. Apparently, they were used to cringing civilians who surrendered immediately, hoping for mercy they probably never received. The driver gaped at them. The three guys in the back blinked and stared. One shook his Kalashnikov like these idiot foreigners didn't get it, as if to say, "Hello, we're armed. Pull over."

Not one of them got the chance to use their guns before Jacob leveled his assault rifle and took out the front tire.

At that speed, the Jeep turned in a sharp skid. Jana jerked the Land Rover to the left to avoid a collision as the driver struggled with the wheel, just managing to keep from flipping. One guy fell out the back, hitting the desert floor hard and rolling over and over.

But Jacob wasn't paying attention to them anymore. He was aiming at the next Jeep in line.

And they were aiming at him.

He let loose a three-round burst just as they opened up.

The shots hit the driver, splashing the interior of the cab with gore. Bullets panged off their Land Rover, punching through the thin outer skin but getting stopped by the bulletproof plating beneath.

Those shots stopped hitting when the second Jeep started swerving, the dead driver falling on the wheel, his buddy next to him grabbing it and desperately trying to keep control.

The Jeep slowed, revealing the two other Jeeps. They'd gotten wise, spread out, and were trying for a pincer movement. One sped up, trying to cut them off. The other slowed, coming around behind, cutting close in front of the second Jeep Jacob had hit.

A storm of bullets came at them. Jana, hunched so low she could barely see above the dashboard, cursed and swerved to get away, driving in a crazy zigzag over the rough desert stones.

This ruined Jacob's aim, so he switched to full auto, spraying the nearest Jeep and hoping to hit something.

That didn't seem to have much of an effect. The two Jeeps kept at them in a full-on chase. A bullet took out the side-view mirror, a fragment of glass cutting Jacob's cheek. Another shot off the door handle.

They're getting too close. Time to change the game.

Jacob's magazine ran out, but with the two Jeeps still bearing down on him, he realized he didn't have time to change it before those guys peppered the whole vehicle with bullets. It was a miracle they hadn't taken him or Jana out yet, or blown a hole right through a tire.

Time for a more radical solution to his problem.

He already had his grenade launcher loaded with a fragmentation grenade, so he aimed at the closer of the two Jeeps and fired.

Just then, Jana drove over a big rock, jerking the Land Rover and making Jacob fly up and hit his head on the ceiling. The grenade sailed over the Jeep to land far off its target.

The explosion did have an effect, though. The two Jeeps immediately veered off. Having half their vehicles already disabled, at least a couple of their guys killed and probably more wounded, and now facing a grenade launcher, the bandits figured there were softer targets out in this wasteland. They did a tight 180 and sped back toward their friends.

Jacob snapped a second magazine into his assault rifle and fired a long burst to send them on their way. Jana was still bouncing the Land Rover through a rough part of the desert, so he doubted any of the bullets hit, but he had made his point. One of the bandit Jeeps had traded a driver for a dead body and started up to join their buddies, while the other vehicle looked truly out of commission. The three Jeeps sped in that direction to pick up the survivors.

Jacob slid back into the seat and reloaded his grenade launcher. Just as he did so, the Land Rover started shaking, each bump worse than the last.

"What the hell?"

"I think we burst a tire," Jana said. "They didn't shoot it out. Must be these rocks we're driving over."

Jacob glanced back at the bandits. They were far behind now but still not out of sight.

"Drive on it anyway."

"Can't for much longer."

"We don't want those guys to think we're disabled."

"What if we burst a second tire? We only have one spare."

"Better than getting shot."

Jana slowed as the Land Rover juddered and shook. Far behind them, the bandits were getting out of the disabled vehicle and moving into other Jeeps.

"I think they busted an axle or something when I took out their tire. They're not trying to replace it."

"We're going to do the same if I keep driving like this."

"See how the land rises a little ahead of us, then dips down? Get over that and we'll be out of sight."

"Let's hope we make it."

The shaking grew worse, accompanied by the telltale slapping sound of a flat tire. The bandits still hadn't left and were too far behind for Jacob to tell what they were doing. Licking their wounds? Preparing for another attack?

They got over the rise and saw nothing but featureless desert beyond for a few miles until a thin strip of green signaled a river in the far distance. Jana slowed the Land Rover to a stop and parked, leaving the engine idling. Jacob hopped out and surveyed the damage. The vehicle was riddled with bullet holes. The back seat was soaked thanks to some rounds piercing the big plastic water jugs they had purchased back in Karachi. The bullets must have come through the windows, ricocheted off the roof, and angled down to hit the jugs.

"Damn. They got all of them."

It was a miracle the same hadn't happened to them.

Jana looked in the back seat. "Wonderful. All we got left is that liter bottle up front."

Jacob grunted. That bottle was half empty. "Let's change this tire and get out of here." He walked around to the back, where the spare was secured, only to find it shredded from bullets. "Aw, crap."

"Don't tell me they got the spare."

"They got the spare. I'm going to check on them. Stay here."

Grabbing a pair of binoculars from the front seat, Jacob jogged up the rise, then got flat on his belly. The sun beat down, and the glare that was reflected off the pale rocks was nearly blinding. Jacob wriggled a few yards more and got behind a rock big enough to hide him. He checked the angle of the sun wouldn't make a reflection off his binoculars and focused them on the bandits.

They looked like they were unloading everything from the disabled Jeep. One guy was on his hands and knees studying the front end, while two others carried the body of the driver to a waiting Jeep. Another lugged a pair of Jerry cans to one of the other vehicles.

Jacob lay still, watching. They finished loading up the Jeep, and all got in the working vehicles. A man stood in the back of one of them, scanning the horizon with a pair of binoculars.

Jacob went prone, counting to a hundred. When he got to seventy, he heard the sound of engines moving away. He counted to a hundred anyway, just in case. Once he looked up again, he saw the Jeeps speeding off into the distance, kicking up clouds of dust as they drove back the way they came.

Jacob watched them until they dwindled into dots, then vanished in a receding haze. He crawled back out of sight, got up, and jogged back to the Land Rover. Jana stood next to it.

"I checked the axle and the hub. Both seem OK," she said.

Jacob grinned. "Good. Now all we need to do is go to the nearest service station. Know where it is?"

"Nope, but I know where we can find people."

She pointed toward the river, miles away. Jacob could make out the faintest haze of smoke hovering above one spot along its course.

"Cooking fires, from the looks of it," Jacob said. "A large farm or maybe a small village. Let's go check it out."

"They might be the base for those bandits."

Jacob nodded. "If it is, then we grab one of their Jeeps. If not, maybe we can get someone to help us."

"Middle Eastern hospitality might not extend to armed strangers in a place like this. It's like a warzone."

"We'll just have to take that chance, unless you want to walk the rest of the way. We had about eight more hours of driving. Not sure what that translates to at marching speed."

"Let's check it out," Jana grumbled.

First, they took out the ruined water jugs from the back, drinking the remnants left on the bottoms of the jugs through the bullet holes. It was so hot that the back seat was almost dry already. Next, they gathered all the weapons, took that last precious half-full liter bottle of water, and headed out.

Jacob worried about leaving the Land Rover out here unguarded but didn't see what they could do about it except try to get back to it as soon as possible.

He surveyed the wide stretch of open desert between them and the village. They both had hats and light clothing, plus half a liter of water. They should get there thirsty but not too dehydrated.

If they got there. The bandits could come back and catch them in the open, in which case they'd be dead in a matter of minutes. Or the villagers could prove hostile, in which case they were stranded. He wouldn't fight some random villagers even if they attacked him. He'd retreat instead. But then they'd be stuck in the middle of nowhere with no help.

Or, as they had feared, the village could be the base for the bandits. If that was true, then they'd be in an uneven fight where the bandits enjoyed superiority in numbers, knew the terrain, and had more maneuverability.

I should have been a mall cop.

"Let's get going," Jana said. "The day's not getting any cooler."

"No. I think it's going to get a lot hotter."

CHAPTER ELEVEN

By the time they made it close enough to the river to smell it, Jana felt like she could drink the entire thing. The featureless desert had played tricks with their eyes, and they had a lot further to walk than they had at first thought.

It had taken at least three hours trudging over rocky, scorching ground to make it to the point where they could clearly see the trees lining the riverbanks and the curl of smoke rising from a score of chimneys.

They still couldn't see the village. It remained hidden behind a line of trees. The faint bleating of goats carried to their ears on the searing air.

Jana felt ragged, the water bottle was long since empty, and she was praying this village proved to be friendly.

That hope vanished when a shot rang out.

Jana and Jacob threw themselves onto the ground. They crawled a little away from each other to make less of a target.

"I think that was a warning shot," Jacob said. "Didn't come close."

A male voice shouted something.

"What did he say?" Jana asked. "I don't speak Urdu."

"Neither do I, but that wasn't Urdu. I think that was Balochi."

"They sent an agent who doesn't speak any of the local languages?"

Jacob shrugged. "That's the federal government for you."

"Try them in Arabic."

Jana could speak it, but they were dealing with a rural village in a conservative province in one of the most conservative countries in the Middle East. In those circumstances, and not many others, she'd let a man speak for her.

Without rising, Jacob raised his head from the dirt a little and cupped a hand to his mouth.

"Do you speak Arabic?" he shouted in that language.

A reply came again in Balochi. Jacob put down his gun and stood.

"What are you doing?" Jana cried.

Jacob waved his empty hands over his head, then dropped prone again.

Another reply in Balochi. Jana got the impression they were being told to wait. One thing she had learned from her command of several languages was that the intonation for many meanings often sounded similar, even in widely different tongues. She hoped she was right and they weren't being told they were about to be skinned alive.

They waited. And waited. Jana checked her watch and saw it had been less than ten minutes, but lying prone on these baking rocks made her feel like a strip of bacon sizzling on a frying pan.

At last they heard another cry from the riverbank, this time an older voice in Arabic.

"Who are you?"

"We are Canadian travelers," Jacob called back. "Our Land Rover lost a tire and we need help. Why did you fire at us?"

"Because you are strangers, and armed. There are bandits here preying on everyone."

Jana let out a gust of relief. They weren't with the bad guys. That didn't mean they'd help, though.

Jacob stood up again, holding out his empty hands.

"We were attacked by those bandits. They damaged our vehicle."

"And you are still alive? How many men did you lose?"

"None."

"Impossible!"

"We're good fighters. We need your help and we can pay."

"If you are enemies of the bandits, you do not need to pay for anything. Come forward. Know that you are being watched by several riflemen. Do not make any hostile moves."

"You shot at us, remember?" Jacob grumbled in English.

Nevertheless, he bent over, picked up his assault rifle, and slung it on his back, holding up his empty hands again. Jana slung her own weapon and wrapped a corner of her yellow headscarf around the lower half of her face.

Together they walked toward the riverbank. As they approached, they spotted several men lying behind rocks or trees, aiming rifles and AK-47s at them. An older man in a white jalwar kemeez stood up and stepped forward a few yards. He had a white brocaded skullcap and a matching beard that came to a point over his heart. Jana took him for the village *ulema*, or religious leader. He had probably learned his Arabic in a madrasa in some nearby town and might be the only person in the village who spoke it well. While every literate person strived to learn how to read Arabic and thus read the Koran, that didn't mean they could hold a conversation.

As they drew closer, a few of the men talked among themselves in Balochi. They sounded surprised, probably about her.

"Are you Peshmerga?" the old man asked.

"No, we're Canadian," Jacob said.

The Peshmerga were Kurdish fighters famous for their fierce female warriors who went toe to toe with ISIS. The TV cameramen loved those good-looking, cocky young women toting assault rifles. Seeing a woman emerging out of the desert laden with firearms, the villagers made the obvious association.

"You do not have to lie to us, young man. We love the Peshmerga. They helped destroy ISIS."

So this was a Shia village. ISIS was Sunni, considered all Shia to be heretics, and vowed to kill every one of them. Foreign relations was not the Islamic State's strong suit.

"I have killed many members of ISIS, my friend," Jacob said, "and I worked with the Peshmerga."

Jana figured that was probably true. She wondered if he had just revealed classified information. Whatever kept them from getting shot at.

They stopped at the edge of the greenery. The men started to come out of hiding. Jana counted about twenty of them, ranging in age from fourteen to sixty, all dressed in the same traditional clothing as their translator, although in more practical browns and greens, faded and patched from long use. A few had AK-47s, and the rest had rifles so old they wouldn't have made the grade to be included in Hashir Khan's bargain bin.

The old man studied him for a moment. "Are you American Special Forces?"

"No."

"CIA? MI6?"

Everyone in this part of the world knew about those organizations, even if they couldn't read a newspaper and had never set foot inside a school.

"We are Canadian travelers, my friend, and there are now at least two or three fewer bandits to worry about."

The old man stared at him, obviously not buying this line.

After a moment, he gestured toward the far side of the river. "Our village is named Sheikh Jibril, after the man who founded it five hundred years ago. You and your Kurdish wife are welcome."

Behind her scarf, Jana smiled. They couldn't imagine a woman other than a Kurd carrying weapons. Well, whatever made them accept her was fine, even though the nearest Peshmerga fighter was probably a thousand miles away.

They joined the village fighters and walked into the shade of the trees. A couple stayed behind as sentries while the rest accompanied them to the river—a shallow run of crystal clear water about ten yards wide that splashed over round stones. Both banks were thick with tall grass, bushes, and trees. Channels had been dug on the far bank to bring the water to the fields beyond the village.

The villagers all asked for translations of what had been said and were soon making small talk with Jacob. While a few snuck glances at Jana walking by his side, most pretended she wasn't even there. That was a sign of respect in this part of the world and something she had never gotten used to.

They crossed a simple bridge of split logs set on large, flat stones just above the surface of the water to the other bank. As they climbed up the bank, Jana enjoying the cool of the shade and moist air after a long, hard slog in the desert, the village came into view.

It was a collection of stone huts with slate roofs. The windows were tiny with wooden shutters, one on each wall. Backyards were enclosed by walls of mudbrick, and for a moment, Jana wondered why they hadn't used the easier building material for the houses too.

The answer quickly came to her—stone walls gave more protection. Those tiny windows could be used as gun ports.

She could see two dusty streets with similar houses along both of them. At the far end of the village stood a minaret made of simple whitewashed mudbrick, a battered loudspeaker hanging from the top so that men working in the fields could hear the call to prayer. While she couldn't see the whole village, she guessed about a hundred homes, maybe five hundred people.

Of those people, no women or children were visible.

"You say your vehicle was damaged?" the ulema asked. "How badly?"

"It's pretty shot up but all we need is a spare tire. It's only a few kilometers from here."

The old man gave some orders in Balochi, and two men hurried off.

"They will get a tractor to tow it back. Go with them. That house right over there is owned by a widow and her children. They would be honored to host your wife. I myself would be honored if you stay with me."

"Thank you," Jacob said. Jana allowed herself to nod.

The ulema had just solved a tricky problem. The rules of hospitality dictated that these strange visitors had to be housed and fed. The rules of propriety meant that a woman could not stay in a house with men in it who weren't her relations. So the widow's house was the best—indeed, only—place to put her. Jacob couldn't stay in a house with a lone woman who wasn't related, so he stayed with the ulema, whose wife was probably of an age when such strictures loosened somewhat, and having her husband present made it safe for her.

By this time, word had spread that there was no danger, and children began to appear in the streets, gathering around to stare at the two strangers and bombard the ulema with questions. Jana smiled at a trio of little girls standing together who couldn't have been more than ten. One of them had a toddler brother in tow and fussed over him while the other two whispered to each other, stared at Jana, and giggled. She smiled again before realizing they couldn't see her face behind the veil she had put over herself, so she added a wink. That got them giggling more. The ulema said something, and one of the two gigglers broke off, took Jana by the hand, and nodded toward the widow's house.

Jana let herself be pulled along, a circle of children surrounding herself and the girl, as the ulema continued to speak to Jacob.

"I thank God you killed some of those bandits. They have attacked us three times in the past month. We have fought them off each time, but they had always managed to take cattle or gasoline. Their attacks are getting fiercer. I think they are angry at our defiance and want to wipe us out."

Oh, crap. I hope they didn't track us here.

As if reading her mind, Jacob said, "You must keep vigilant then."

"We always do. Come, you must be tired. We will find you shelter."

CHAPTER TWELVE

Jana sat cross-legged on a red and white carpet of a hypnotically complex design, a tea cup and an array of dishes spread before her. The girl sat next to her, bombarding her with questions in Balochi while a smaller brother and sister sat nearby, openmouthed and staring. Their widowed mother, who didn't look more than twenty-five, smiled shyly and gestured for her to eat. An old woman sat next to her, trying to focus on her through milky cataracts.

The interior of the house was simple, with no furniture except for a large wooden chest and three charpai in the next room that served as a bedroom. A photo that hung on the wall showed a young man and the widow, looking nervous and very young, perhaps on their wedding day.

Jana had been sitting here an hour, unable to have a conversation with her hosts, and had been thoroughly enjoying herself.

While they didn't share a language, they communicated well enough. The girl eagerly showed her a loom in the backyard set in the shade of a brush awning. A half-completed rug was stretched on it, every bit as complex as the one in the house. The girl sat down and worked the loom for a minute, a pattern on the carpet slowly expanding, and indicated that she and her mother sold the rugs to houses all over the village and beyond.

That made Jana feel a bit better. This little family had a source of income, although probably a meager one. She wished she could get one of their rugs into a carpet shop in Europe. It would sell for thousands, more than this family saw in a couple of years. The Balochis were famous for their rugs.

Jana ate while they watched. She couldn't get her hosts to eat with her, although she managed to give the smaller two children a couple of dates, which they chewed slowly without taking their eyes off this strange apparition in their home.

While Jana had been a foreigner in many Middle Eastern homes before, she had never been in a home this remote. She might have been the first Western woman these people had ever seen in real life instead of television. Her clothing, her physical features, everything about her was different than what they were used to. The 9mm pistol and walkie talkie on her belt, and the assault rifle leaning on the wall behind her, didn't exactly help her blend in either.

As she ate some more bread and dates, her eyes wandered up to that photo again, wondering what had happened to the young man in the portrait, who had died and left a young widow and three fatherless children.

The widow saw her looking and gestured at the photo, her mouth turned down. Then she gestured out toward the desert, made the sound of an engine, and formed her fingers into a gun. The girl beside her sniffled and wiped away a tear. Her younger siblings, too little to understand what was going on, continued munching on their dates.

Jana rubbed the girl's back and gave her mother a sympathetic look. So he had died protecting his village, protecting them.

From outside, she heard the screech of feedback on a bad sound system, then an anxious voice shouting something over a loudspeaker. The one from the mosque? The widow and her eldest daughter sat bolt upright, going pale. The old woman put a hand to her ear and asked a question. The announcer continued, shouting something over and over again. The eldest girl ran to her mother and burst into tears. The widow clung to her and rocked her back and forth.

An attack. It must be.

Jana grabbed her assault rifle and stood, knocking over her teacup. Everyone looked at her, terrified and fascinated at the same time.

She made it to the front door as the first shots cracked the air.

Running out into the street, she came upon chaos. Old people were grabbing children and leading them indoors. Men, many of whom looked like they had just run in from the fields, hurried into homes and emerged carrying guns.

Jana looked around, unsure where to go and unable to ask anyone.

More shots rang out. They came from the south and east. To the east was the river and the desert out of which they had walked. She didn't know what lay to the south.

She ran south, joining three men who gripped old rifles, their faces set with grim determination, eyes sparking with fear. They did a doubletake when she joined them, and Jana realized she hadn't covered her face. Too bad. There were more important things to think about right now than the rules of propriety.

In a small town square near the widow's house, she spotted the Land Rover hitched to an old tractor. Why hadn't Jacob radioed her to tell her he was back? She stopped by the Land Rover and pulled out her walkie talkie.

"Jacob, where are you?"

The gunfire on both sides of the village increased in tempo. Jacob didn't answer.

"Jacob, do you read me?"

More firing, nearly drowned out by the *thud thud thud* of a heavy machine gun.

Jana swore. They didn't have a gun like that, and the villagers wouldn't either, so the bandits must have brought up stronger reinforcements.

The noise came from the south. Cursing, Jana ran to catch up with the three men still running in that direction.

A cry to her left made her turn. She saw the ulema, gripping a rifle that looked as old as he was, running across the makeshift bridge, waving for a couple of armed and gangly teenagers hurrying to catch up with him.

Jana continued to run south. The houses began to peter out, and she came to a more open area of fields fed by narrow irrigation canals to her right. Straight ahead was a dirt track running alongside the river. It led south, perhaps linking up with that track they had been on when they got attacked.

A low stone wall marked the end of the village, running from the river's edge to the track. On the other side of the track stood a sturdy, two-story stone structure and a wall that continued to the right to link up with the wall around the field.

That building was getting hammered by gunfire. A few villagers crouched behind the building and wall to the right of the track, occasionally popping up to fire a round or two at the enemy beyond that she still couldn't see. No one was posted at the wall between the track and the riverbank.

Ducking low, she ran behind the house, then moved along it to the right to get to the wall. A middle-aged villager with a Kalashnikov stared at her for a moment before rising up to fire a three-round burst at the attackers.

Jana looked at the same time. In the distance, she could see two of the Jeeps that had pursued them before, idling about two hundred yards away.

In between was a third Jeep, its bed occupied by a heavy machine gun protected by a large rectangular steel plate. It was putting down a constant fire that smacked into the wall of the building. Anyone inside had to hide. If they revealed themselves at a window to return fire, they would have been dead in an instant.

The altered Jeep was called a "Technical" in this part of the world. Take any Jeep with good suspension and add a heavy weapon on the back, and you have some serious mobile firepower. A poor man's infantry fighting vehicle. At least they didn't have a cannon on the thing, or the village's defenses would crumble in a few minutes.

They might be bringing something like that up.

Men fired from the other two Jeeps as well, spraying the area with their Kalashnikovs. They didn't try to advance.

Why aren't they advancing?

Jana thought she knew. She needed to check, though.

She burst through the heavy wooden door into the building to find the ground floor was filled with sacks of grain. She immediately ducked when she saw an open window in front of her, just in time to avoid a burst of bullets pouring through the space to hit the rock wall behind her. The bullets ricocheted off the wall, one planting in the dirt floor by her foot, others thumping into the grain sacks or the wooden rafters.

Four men hunkered behind two open windows, a mixture of teenagers and senior citizens. One was already injured in the leg by what must have been another ricochet. Jacob was not among them.

Spotting a narrow set of wooden steps on the far side of the room, she crawled there and raced up it.

Upstairs housed farm equipment, and there were four more men up there firing out another pair of windows. As she made it up, they ducked down, the heavy machine gun raking the side of the building. Jacob wasn't here, either.

But there was something else she needed—a side window facing the river.

She opened the thick wooden shutter and peeked out.

From this vantage point, she could see the river sparkling in the sunshine. She didn't get a good view of either bank, though. The far one was partially obscured by reeds and trees, and the vegetation and the slope on the near bank made that side even harder to make out.

More bullets smacked against the stone wall. One bullet made it through to ricochet off the back wall.

She raced over to the front window to dare a peek. The three vehicles remained at long range, not having moved at all in the time since she last checked. She also didn't see any infantry with them using the heavy machine gun as cover for their advance.

That's because they're advancing along the river. This covering fire is just a distraction.

Do the villagers have anyone guarding the river?

She rushed to the side window again, searching for shapes in the brush. Either the villagers were very well hidden, or they weren't there.

"Hey!" she shouted at the men trying to fire at the vehicles without getting their heads blown off.

They stared at her. She pointed out the window toward the river. Then at the enemy position, and drew her finger in the direction of the village.

Their blank faces showed they didn't understand. A moment later, they all had to duck as another burst of bullets scoured the outside wall.

She repeated the motion, then raised her hand in a question.

Again they didn't seem to understand.

She pointed at two of them, then at herself, and pointed at the river.

Without waiting for a response, she rushed to the stairs and went down.

Once there, she pointed to another man, the one with the best gun, pointed to herself, and pointed to the river. Then she ran outside.

Now came the tough part. From the side of the building to the beginning of the wall on the other side of the dirt road was a good ten feet of open, unprotected space. It looked like ten miles.

She backed up a little, keeping behind the building, then ran for it. By the time she appeared in the open space, she was sprinting, almost doubled over to make less of a target.

She got halfway across before the bandits could react. Then the air filled with bullets. Dirt stung her legs as bullets hit the ground all around her.

She dove for the wall, tucked into a roll, and rolled as shots chased her all the way to shelter. From there, she crawled to the far end of the wall, where it stopped just before the steep riverbank.

Glancing over her shoulder to try and communicate with the men she'd gathered, she found they hadn't followed her. They hadn't even come out of the building.

She turned back toward the riverbank, scanning the underbrush on either side of the water. For a moment, she saw nothing, then a shadow on the far side of the river flitted from one clump of greenery to the next.

Someone was advancing on the village not fifty yards from her position.

Another movement caught her eye, this time on the near bank, and only thirty yards from her position. She had been right. The bandits were laying down distraction fire while some of their comrades worked their way up the undefended riverbank.

There were probably villagers around the bridge further back at the center of the village, but that was too far. The bandits could flank the building unopposed, cut down the defenders, and then the Technical and the two Jeeps could roll right into the village.

And Jana was the only one around to stop them.

CHAPTER THIRTEEN

Jana went prone, using the wall to one side and the rough riverbank to her front as cover.

She waited for someone to make a move.

She didn't have to wait long.

A figure crept through the rushes on the near bank, crouched low, peering all around as he advanced. Jana could not see him clearly. She watched down the sights of her assault rifle, heart hammering in her chest.

She was about to kill again, something she hated, something she kept getting forced into, something necessary.

She thought of that young widow who had shown her so much hospitality even though she had so little to give. What would happen to her if the bandits took over the village? What would happen to the children after the bandits left, probably taking their mother with her, as well as all the food?

Jana couldn't let that happen. These raiders were here by their own choice, and by their own choice, they would be killed.

But first, she had to determine that this figure creeping through the rushes was really a raider and not some villager.

The man darted across a clear patch, and in the second that Jana saw him clearly, she saw he was dressed in a new jalwar chemeez, army boots instead of the villagers' sandals, and carried a brand new AK-47.

Plus, he was advancing, scanning the area for hidden foes, not retreating to someplace familiar.

Jana waited for her opportunity. The man had paused in a cluster of rushes, but beyond that position lay a more open area. He'd probably go prone and crawl behind the cover of a few large rocks scattered just beyond his position. She aimed for the edge of the rushes. She could see him as a vague shape inside the growth but didn't want to lose the element of surprise by firing half blind and perhaps missing.

She lost it anyway when another bandit appeared on the far bank, spotted her, and let out a cry.

Jana flicked the fire selector lever to a three-round burst and fired into the rushes. Then she shifted her aim to the man on the far bank, who fired at her on automatic, the rounds chewing up the riverbank just below her position. She kept her head and fired a burst at him.

Missed. He ducked back behind a tree. Jana fired another burst and missed again. The man curled up behind the tree and made an almost impossible target.

She switched to single fire to get a more accurate shot. The flare of a rifle from the far bank a bit to the right of the tree showed the guy had backup. She focused on the guy behind the tree. When he showed himself to take another shot, Jana fired. He flinched and fell back, either wounded or killed, Jana couldn't see which.

The other man on the far bank fired again, the bullet humming over Jana's head. She also saw movement in the rushes on the nearby bank. She had only wounded that one.

She wriggled back out of sight, shifted a bit to the left, then popped up on one knee to fire two shots in rapid succession at the half-obscured man on the near bank. The raider on the far bank fired just as she dropped back down, the bullet missing her by inches.

She was pretty sure she had taken out her latest target, leaving only the rifleman on the far bank uninjured.

And whoever might be coming up behind him. The gang would have sent more than three guys along this riverbed. These three were only the advanced scouts.

The cover fire from the Technical and two Jeeps continued. They were waiting for the assault to flank the building so they could advance.

She switched to automatic, popped up again, and hosed the far bank until she had emptied her magazine. Then she dropped back out of sight, switched to a fresh magazine, and crawled back toward the village. She was too exposed in this position.

After about twenty yards, she found a spot on the riverbank where a tree grew right out of its side, a cluster of bushes all around it. This would give cover as she slid down the slope to the river.

Just as she was preparing to get down there, the sound of movement behind her made her turn.

The three guys she had tried to communicate with in the building crouched behind her. They must have looked out of the side window and seen the danger.

"Nice of you to join me."

They grinned and said something in Balochi.

They were all young men, one with a Kalashnikov and the other two with halfway decent hunting rifles. She nodded to them and scrambled down the slope, ending up in a thicket running all the way to the water's edge.

The firing from the desert to the east, the other pincer of the bandits' attack, had drawn closer. She heard the thud of a grenade.

Nothing she could do about that right now. She had her hands full with the menace coming up the river.

Peering through the gaps in the greenery, she spotted movement on both banks. She switched to single fire. The enemy was at too long of a range to waste bullets on bursts or full auto.

She felt a presence beside and behind her. Turning, Jana found her three companions had silently joined her, looking down the river in the direction of the threat.

Their eyes all went wide at the same time.

Jana spun around and saw a group of bandits on their side of the river advancing out of the brush. On the other bank, a group rushed up the slope. One carried a rocket-propelled grenade.

She aimed at the guy with the RPG, who was obviously trying to get into position to blow a hole in the side of the building and force any survivors to flee. If he managed to, those vehicles would drive right in here, and it would all be over.

Her shot missed. She fired again as he scrambled up the last few feet of slope.

Again she missed. His buddies on both sides of the river returned fire, the bullets whickering through the bushes and thwacking into trees. Her companions fired back, the reports of their gunshots throbbing in her eardrums.

The guy with the RPG crested the riverbank. In another moment, he would be out of sight.

Jana let out a breath, forced herself to relax, and squeezed the trigger. The man, now on the far bank and only visible from the waist up, jerked and fell.

His RPG dropped out of sight.

There were five guys on the slope behind him. One was already down from a villager's gunshot. The other four saw what happened to their point man. One shouted to the others and ran up the slope as the three covered him.

Jana took him out with a single shot.

One of the villagers took out another man on the slope, and the remaining two made a break for it, desperate to get to the RPG and out of the killing zone.

Jana dropped one before he made it to the top. The other, cringing and zigzagging, made it up and over and out of sight.

"Damn it!"

In a few moments, he would have made it to a good firing position and would be aiming at the house.

Fire increased at their front. The bandits on their side of the river had gone prone, hiding behind rocks and fallen logs, and poured fire into their position. One of the young farmers cried out, clutching his shoulder.

Jana stayed low, casting nervous glances at the far bank, where the man who retrieved the RPG would be setting up right this moment.

She had to stop him.

Switching to full auto, she rose up, a roar tearing out of her throat. She sprinted for the other side of the river, splashing through the shallow water, spraying fire at the enemy.

Running over rough terrain while firing on full auto at a half-concealed enemy is no way to hit anything, but it did make them duck for cover.

Jana ran out of bullets just as she made it to the far bank.

She got halfway up the slope before they started firing back.

Bullets thumped into the earth close by her. She dodged behind a tree, then worked her way up the rest of the slope. A hot lance across her inner right arm made her hiss with pain.

She made it up and over and out of sight of the gunmen in the riverbed.

The raider with the RPG, wearing camo pants over a loose shirt and a wicked grin spread across his unshaven face, knelt not five yards away, aiming his RPG at the side of the building. His AK-47 was slung across his back. A carrier bag with three more rounds lay in front of him. No fire came from the building's side window. Those inside were unaware of the danger.

The raider was just about to fire when he spotted Jana. For a second, both froze. Jana was out of ammo, and he was carrying a weapon that, at this range, would kill him just as much as it would kill her.

Jana tossed her assault rifle at him just as he dropped the RPG.

The barrel smacked him on the side of the head, making him fumble as he tried to unsling his assault rifle.

Jana drew her pistol, flicked off the safety, and leveled it at him just a half second after he brought his AK-47 to bear.

She had the sickening feeling that he'd get to fire first.

CHAPTER FOURTEEN

Jacob sprinted along the riverbank, desperate to get into the fight on the south side of the village. The wound to his side he had sustained in Morocco burned. He ignored it. When the alarm went out for an attack, he had naturally rushed across the river to fend off an attack coming out of the desert from the direction where they had first encountered the bandits.

There he had found a ragged line of raiders advancing under cover of a Technical fitted with a heavy machine gun. A few other vehicles were parked in the distance, out of range. While the villagers engaged the raiders, he had wormed his way along a little gully to get close to the Technical.

That had nearly gotten him killed. The raiders had noticed the gully, too, and three of them had snuck along its length straight into him. They now lay dead at the bottom of the gully.

A minute later, he had gotten to a good position on the Technical's flank and readied his grenade launcher.

The sight of the fireball and the crew's shredded bodies flying into the air had taken the fight out of the raiders, and they began to withdraw, firing as they went, taking more casualties from the villagers and Jacob.

As much as he'd have liked to pursue those guys to their waiting vehicles and blow some of those up, too, increasing fire to the south of the village told him the battle wasn't won yet.

So he had retraced his steps along the gully and ran along the riverbank to where villagers and a group of raiders, each hiding in a cluster of rushes by the riverbank, were exchanging fire. The rattle of another Technical somewhere on the road to the village told him of an even bigger danger.

Jacob was just about to cross the river and engage it when one of the men on the far bank pointed to his side of the river and shouted something in Balochi. It sounded urgent.

Jacob hesitated a split second, then ran up the riverbank. These guys might be untrained, but they knew what was going on in this sector more than he did. He had to trust them.

Just before getting to the top of the riverbank, he went prone and crawled up the rest, keeping low.

He made it just in time to see Jana drop her PK-21 assault rifle and pull out her pistol. Nearby crouched a bandit who had just dropped an RPG and was unslinging an AK-47.

Jacob could tell the raider was going to win this game of fast draw.

He aimed, but Jana was partially in the way and shifting her body as she readied her pistol.

He couldn't shoot without a good fifty-fifty chance of hitting Jana.

Just then, salvation came from an unlikely source.

One of the villagers, so young his attempt at a beard looked like some lint had gotten stuck to his chin, popped up from the riverbank and fired a rifle, taking the man with the RPG straight through the heart.

Jana flinched, let out a gust of air, gave him a thumb's up, and picked up her assault rifle again.

Jacob ran up to her.

"What's the situation?"

"A Technical and two Jeeps trying to get past the building. This guy was part of a flanking movement to take out the building."

"We'll switch it up on them," Jacob said, grabbing the dead man's RPG and satchel with the spare rounds.

Jacob motioned for the villager and his two buddies to get out of the riverbed and move around the flank of the group of raiders in the rushes. Shooting down, they'd have a good chance of taking them out. Once they were moving into position, Jacob and Jana rushed back a bit, descended into the riverbank again, and sprinted across. A few bullets came their way from the bandits in the brush, but none passed close.

They scrambled up the far slope and hurried to the stretch of wall on this side of the dusty lane.

Jacob peeked over the wall, estimated the range of the three vehicles, and adjusted the sights on the RPG.

"I'll cover you," Jana said.

They rose up in unison. Jacob fired at the Technical while Jana fired a burst at the vehicles.

The rocket-propelled grenade slammed into the Technical's engine block, sending shreds of the hood and chunks of engine parts tearing into the crew. A split second later, the fuel lines caught, igniting the gas tank.

The ensuing fireball was enough to make several of the fighters in the backs of the Jeeps flanking it to jump out and run away. Immediately both drivers got their Jeeps into gear and began to turn around.

Jacob hurried to load another round. As he did, fire from the building showed the villagers were getting back into the game. Now that they weren't being hosed with heavy caliber rounds, they could actually take the time to aim. Sparks flew off the righthand Jeep as bullets hit it all over. The Jeep jerked and ground to a stop, the driver slumping over the wheel, the last of the crew hopping out and sprinting for safety.

The other Jeep was getting away, though, driving off in a plume of dust and gathering speed.

Jacob stood, aimed, and fired.

The rocket-propelled grenade flew across the intervening space to take the Jeep in the back of the cab, blowing it right off the chassis. The Jeep, now without a driver or even a steering wheel, slowly ground to a stop.

The few remaining raiders ran out of range.

Within a few seconds, the most awe-inspiring sound of battle filled the air—silence.

Jacob heard nothing, but the ringing in his own ears and the occasional crack of a firearm as a villager thought he saw movement or decided on one last parting shot at extreme long range.

But soon, those shots died away, and Jacob heard nothing but the ringing in his own ears. He and Jana crawled to the riverbank and found that the group of raiders there were all dead or had fled; the villagers picked through their bodies.

Jacob scanned the riverbed and the desert beyond and could see no survivors from the attack. A few writhed in their death throes, soon to be dispatched by the villagers they had intended to victimize. He stood and looked back at the burning or disabled vehicles on the road. No survivors there, either.

It was over.

Then a new sound broke the silence.

Cheering.

Cheers came from the building, from the riverbed, and from the desert beyond. As the cheers rose, they were soon accompanied by the trilling of the women, who all emerged from the houses that usually shielded them from view to call out their exultation at being saved.

Children ran around the streets, jumping up and down and cheering too. A little boy gave him a very American high five he must have seen on television.

Jacob's heart swelled with satisfaction.

The ulema came racing up to them and embraced Jacob.

"Thank you! We couldn't have done it without you and your wife!"

"You're welcome. You gave us shelter in a hostile land, it was the least we could do."

The group that Jana had led from the riverbed came running up, all of them speaking at the same time in Balochi. The ulema calmed them down and asked the eldest to speak. After a minute, he turned back to Jacob.

"They say your wife fought like a man. She saw the danger of the raiders sneaking up beside the storage building to blow it apart. We would have lost the battle if it wasn't for her."

"She was proud to fight beside your men," Jacob said.

He gave his companion a sidelong look. She did not appear happy to be talked about like she wasn't there but nevertheless understood that this was how the society was in rural Pakistan. Men and women stayed separate.

Not that she had to stay alone. A group of veiled women and unveiled girls came rushing up to her, embracing her and sending up a loud trilling. They moved as a group with a smiling Jana at the center back toward the village.

Jacob laughed, then turned to the ulema.

"We need to secure the village perimeter. Send out men in groups of four to make sure there are no raiders pretending to be dead. Take their guns, ammo, and any other useful equipment. They're yours now."

The ulema smiled. "That will make us much stronger. This band of thieves will think twice before coming at us again. Them or any other group."

His smile vanished as he heard wailing coming from the village. A young man came up to him and said something. The ulema turned to Jacob.

"God gives and God takes. We have lost four neighbors today. Five more are injured."

"Is there a hospital nearby?" Jacob asked, dreading the answer.

"There is one in a town two hours drive away. I fear they might not make it, or we might be attacked on the road."

“Take me to them. I have a medical kit in my Land Rover. I’ll see what I can do.”

The ulema put a hand on his shoulder. “You know how to save lives as well as take them? God has given you many talents.”

Jacob grimaced. “I’m a bit better at taking life than giving.”

“Perhaps you haven’t been trying hard enough.”

“Perhaps.”

Perhaps I haven’t been trying at all. Time to start.

He ran to get his medical kit.

CHAPTER FIFTEEN

Jana hated to leave the village. It was the next morning, and in observance of Muslim tradition, the dead had already been buried. Muslim funerals were simple affairs. The dead men were wrapped in winding sheets and put in graves that lacked names or dates. While their heroism and sacrifice meant they would be remembered for generations, their souls had left their bodies, and thus their bodies were not worth much more ceremony other than a wash and a quick prayer.

The mourning of the village did not keep Jana from being treated like royalty. A steady succession of women and girls knocked on their hosts' door to come to see the female warrior, and while she couldn't understand what they said, she knew they were thanking and admiring her with all their hearts.

She wished she could stay and train the women to fight, to better defend themselves the next time a bandit group decided to raid. But she knew the men of the village would never allow it. Balochi women weren't foreign women and were not permitted to do things that they could get away with. It was unfair, and in a dangerous region like this, it was impractical, but there it was.

There was no time anyway. After spending half the night patching up the wounded and nursing one bad case from the brink of death, Jacob had set out for the nearest town with several heavily armed villagers in a couple of cars. He had returned with a pair of used Land Rover tires and fitted the least worn one onto the car, keeping the older one as a spare.

Time to depart. She had packed up her gear and started saying her final farewells to the village women. The two youngest children, both toddlers, had warmed up to her, shrugging off her weirdness after a short time the way children do. Their mother hugged her warmly and pressed a bag of food into her hands. The daughter, who had taken her here on their first day in the village, burst into tears and gave her a big hug.

Jana kissed her on the cheek. The girl kissed her back and, stepping back, pulled off her bracelet of glass beads and tried to put it on Jana's wrist, only to find it didn't fit. The girl rushed out to the loom, returned with a bit of thread, and rethreaded the bracelet for a bigger size. Once it was on Jana's wrist, they embraced again. Jana felt around her pockets for something to give her back and couldn't find anything other than guns, ammo, and other military gear.

A sudden idea came to her. Rummaging around her pack, she pulled out a pair of binoculars. The girl gasped, and everyone gathered around to look at them. Jana led her to the yard, adjusted the binoculars to fit her narrower face, and showed her how to focus. The girl squealed with delight. In an instant, she had raced up a ladder leading to the rooftop and stood up there, slowly turning in a circle to study the horizon.

Jana watched, surprised at the quick transformation from a kid getting a gift to a serious adult. And then she realized she had taught at least one girl how to help defend the village.

The kid was checking if the bandits were coming back.

Jana, her mother, and a couple of neighbor women stood in the yard, watching the girl as she studied every inch of the horizon.

After a long moment, the girl turned to them and smiled, saying something in Balochi. Her mother said something back; the girl nodded and went back to studying the horizon.

A new game for the village girls. Too damn serious of one, but they have a serious life.

After another round of goodbyes and hugs, Jana headed out to the waiting Land Rover, where Jacob was talking with a circle of village men. They got in, said their goodbyes, and after receiving more gifts of food than they could possibly eat, waved and drove off.

Jana poked her head out the window and looked back. Sure enough, that girl was still up on her roof, checking for bandits. Then she turned their direction. Jana waved and, even at this distance, could see when the girl's face cracked into a smile. She waved back, and the two kept on waving to each other until the village disappeared in the distance.

***

The sun was slanting low in a hazy sky before they made it to the dig site. The sky and bare mountains turned the same shade of salmon as they passed a little village their map said was Zaranka, its houses and mosque looking much like the dusty lowland village they had risked their lives to defend.

For much of the day, Jana had taken over the wheel, speeding through the featureless desert and keeping a sharp eye out while Jacob slept. He had spent the entire previous evening playing medic and deserved a rest.

Jana had glanced at him several times as he lay back in his seat, his head bouncing with every bump, mouth slack. Not the prettiest picture, but Jana remembered how he had been with the patients, working diligently, trying to reassure them, and doing everything in his power to save them.

And he had.

But when the lowlands gave way to rough foothills and winding mountain roads, Jana had woken him up and had him drive. The way to the dig site was through a maze of unmarked tracks, and only he had memorized the specific location.

They approached a bluff overlooking the village, the Land Rover bouncing over a rough track. Jana worried about the used tire they'd bought, which had a slow leak. They had to stop twice at gas stations along the way to pump air into it. At one, they had lucked out and been able to replace their windows. It had kept them from sucking in a few pounds each of sand.

"The villagers are sure to have spotted us," Jana said. "A Land Rover with a bunch of bullet holes doesn't exactly blend in around here."

"Yeah, I was thinking about that," Jacob said, gripping the wheel and looking around. "In the lowlands they could all tell we had tangled with bandits. The guy who fixed our windows didn't even bat an eye. I'm sure it wasn't the first vehicle he'd seen riddled with bullets. Up here, there are no bandit gangs. The clans are in control, and they keep watch. As you can see, there are farmhouses all over this area. We stick out, but at least we can move relatively fast. If we approached in foot, we'd stick out more and take longer to get there and back."

Jana nodded. The concerned medic of the night before had vanished, replaced by the keyed-up veteran.

Jacob went on. "There's another road on the other side of this bluff. It goes past a few large farmhouses and then into another valley and down to the lowlands. We'll go out there so we don't use the same road twice."

"Always be unpredictable in your movements," Dad used to tell her. *"Keep your enemies guessing."*

He had told her this when she was fifteen when her only enemy was an arrogant girl named Carla Engels, the petty leader of a snobby little clique in her high school who tried to exclude Jana from the social circle. Carla had been annoying but hardly a threat to her life.

She wondered where Carla was now—probably living in some boring suburb with a couple of bratty kids.

Thoughts of her father made her take out the fake business card she had discovered in a Moroccan safe house. A Pakistani taxi service with three phone numbers that didn't exist. What could it mean? She stared at it for a minute, not finding any answers, and put it back in her pocket.

The Land Rover bounced up a steep incline before leveling off and stopping. Jana took in a sharp breath. Spread out in front of her was an extensive archaeological site with a test trench and several excavation squares.

They got out. A breeze blew across the top of the bluff, rustling the tarpaulins protecting the excavated areas. An unseen bird twittered somewhere nearby.

"Robert and Oscar were grabbed right after they brought down a spy drone searching this area," Jacob said. "Robert generally manned the drone, so I'm thinking it was him who saved the data on a thumb drive and hid it somewhere."

"How do you know the Balochistan government didn't get it?"

"Because they haven't presented it as evidence. Sure, they wouldn't want to show off what Robert and Oscar found, but they could show a little footage, something not sensitive or at least not too sensitive, to prove their point."

"I guess it wasn't in there," Jana said, pointing to a toolshed on the other end of the bluff. The padlock had been broken and lay in two pieces on the ground, along with a scattering of tools. The door creaked forlornly in the breeze.

"Too obvious. Robert might have hidden it in one of these pits."

"They're called excavation squares."

"Whatever."

Jacob started pulling off tarps. Jana helped him and gasped when she saw what they covered.

An entire town had once stood atop this bluff. The test trench cut through several buildings, their stone foundations showing up clearly. Various features, such as hearths and storage pits, were clearly delineated. The test trench had even cut into the edge of a well. The excavators had dug down three meters into the silted up well before giving up.

While she wasn't an expert on the region's archaeology, the remains of a couple of pots stuck in the base and unexcavated side of the test trench suggested this was early, perhaps from the Indus Valley Civilization. This would make it an outlying settlement since that culture built its settlements mostly on the easily irrigated lowlands near rivers. Maybe it was a local culture that imported Indus Valley ware and other cultural elements.

Jacob pulled away a tarp from a nearby excavation square cut beside a promising section of the test trench. Jana hurried over.

She saw why they had expanded here. The foundations cutting through the trench at this spot were more substantial, indicating an important building. The square had revealed part of the entrance, with a column base flanking a doorway. The rest of the doorway and matching column remained buried.

"Were your colleagues archaeologists? This excavation is actually pretty well done."

"Really?"

"Well, I would have added another square over there to fully excavate that feature that looks like it might be a forge, but yeah, they did OK."

"Robert is a quick study. His real passion besides fighting terror is learning languages. Makes you and me look barely literate. The guy has a natural talent. He used to learn languages just by sitting with a book in that language and a dictionary. No grammar, no native speaker to hang out with. He'd just sit and learn it. Then ask a native speaker for pronunciation. Or he'd do it the other way, going to a place where he didn't speak the local lingo and just bumbling along for a few weeks before becoming fluent. I've never seen anything like it."

Jana went over to another excavation square, one well away from the test trench. She didn't see why they had chosen that particular spot. Perhaps they had seen something promising on the surface that they had subsequently pulled away.

She pulled away the tarp and froze.

What lay beneath was simply too good to be true.

CHAPTER SIXTEEN

"Amazing!" Jana's cry made Jacob turn from the square on the other end of the excavation that he was studying.

"What is it?" he asked as he ran over.

Once he got there, all he saw was the base of a thick stone wall with a bunch of squiggles carved onto it below a series of carved dancing figures jammed up against the dirt edge of the square.

"What?" he asked again.

Jana pointed a trembling finger at the squiggles.

"D-do you know what this means?"

"Eat at Joe's?"

"You are such an idiot."

"So I'm told."

"This is Harappan writing."

"Okay."

"As in the Indus Valley Civilization."

"Oay."

Jana managed to tear her eyes off the writing long enough to give him one of her scolding looks, then went back to admiring the squiggles.

"So … what does it mean?" he asked sheepishly.

"What it means is that your buddies have the most incredible beginner's luck. This is the longest Harappan inscription ever found."

"This? It's only got like fifty symbols."

"Yeah. The Harappan script is only found with a few symbols at most, and usually on stamp seals or pottery. The longest inscription ever found is half the length of this one, and I've never heard of an inscription on the stone wall of a building before. This is unprecedented!"

Jana pulled out her phone and started taking pictures.

"So what does it say?"

"I don't know. Nobody knows. The script has never been deciphered, mostly because we have so few examples of it. This might be the key to break the code."

Break the code ...

Robert had loved codes as much as he loved languages.

Jacob noticed the wall on which the inscription was written was set a bit out from the wall of the excavation square, leaving a narrow space behind it.

He jumped in into the square.

"Careful!" Jana said.

He ignored her, pushing his fingers into the space, setting off a trickle of soil from the dirt wall of the excavation square.

"CAREFUL!"

"It's made of stone," Jacob said, feeling around in the space and wondering what kind of poisonous creatures might lurk in Pakistan's dark, cool spaces. "I'm not going to hurt it. Crap!"

The stone shifted forwards, breaking loose from the stones behind it. He caught it before it toppled over.

"I told you to be careful!"

Now that the space had widened, he could reach in further, fingers probing along the soil and pebbles until they wrapped around the cool metal of a thumb drive.

"Bingo."

"Do you always say 'bingo' when you wreck priceless discoveries?"

Jacob grinned, holding up the thumb drive. "I didn't wreck it at all!"

"Very funny. Put the stone back. No, wait. I'll do it. You'll only mess it up."

She jumped into the square, grasped the stone with both hands and pushed Jacob aside with her hip. She gently put the stone back in place, then took a couple of closeup photos of each of the symbols.

"Done?" Jacob asked. "We need to get out of here."

He was looking out over the village of Zaranka to one side and the farmhouses to the other. Local men had come out to stare.

She hopped out of the square and took a look around.

"Yeah. Good idea."

"Glad to see your instinct for survival trumps your love of archaeology."

They resisted the urge to run to the Land Rover. They didn't want to look any more suspicious than they already did.

Jacob got behind the wheel and headed down the back side of the bluff, along a dirt track that led past several farmhouses and, eventually, his map told him, to a gravel road that would take them to the nearest town. From there, they could get on a highway leading to Karachi, call Orhan, and get the hell out of there.

"Once we get along the road a few miles, we need to check out that thumb drive," he told Jana. "I brought a computer with a decoder and satellite uplink. We can send the intel directly back to the nearest field station."

"What were they looking for?"

"That's classified."

"Everything you do is classified. Stop being annoying and tell me."

Jacob flashed her a grin. "Annoying? I thought I was charming."

"No, just annoying," she said without heat. "And the next time we need to handle a priceless artifact, let me do it. Now what were your buddies looking for?"

"Militant camps funded by the provincial government. The new folks in charge are putting their fingers in a whole lot of pies."

"What does Islamabad think of that?"

"The national government probably doesn't know, and if Washington decides to share that intel with them, there's going to be hell to pay."

"That would be just the excuse Islamabad would need to shut the whole Shia movement down."

"Yup."

Jacob drove past the first farmhouse, a walled compound with a couple of buildings inside, visible only by their roofs. A boy watched over a herd of goats on a patch of scrub, and beyond that were some cultivated terraces fed by a mountain stream.

They descended and soon came to another compound similar to the first, except no one was in sight.

"Looks like we made it," Jacob said, keeping a sharp eye out. "I guess they decided not to watch this place. They might have paid one of the locals to put in a call if they see anything suspicious, though. Once we get to that gravel road way down in the valley over there I'm going to floor it. We'll have to risk the tire."

"We have a spare, but I wouldn't want to go on anything but pavement with that old thing."

"No kidding, I—"

Jacob's words got cut off by a sudden movement to their left. Several uniformed figures had risen up in unison above the compound wall. Usually, there was no way up on either side. They had obviously set up ladders or boxes.

And their intention was clear from their guns.

"Duck!" he shouted.

Jacob floored it and followed his own advice.

For the second time that week, their Land Rover got peppered with bullets, every window spiderwebbing within the first couple of seconds. Jacob kept driving blind. He didn't dare poke his head up. At least the armor plating was keeping the bullets out, assuming these guys didn't pull out an RPG.

Straight ahead ran a long, relatively straight open road, providing the attackers with the perfect target opportunity. He needed to do something rash. Now.

Jacob waited until he thought he'd gone far enough and swung the Land Rover to the left. He gritted his teeth, half expecting to slam into the compound wall, but he had guessed right, and he swung around the corner. The firing died away.

He peeked over the dashboard. They were driving along the front of the compound, right past the metal gate.

"Get ready to bail!" he shouted, slamming on the brakes. Jana had already grabbed her assault rifle.

They skidded to a halt in a plume of dust and jumped out. Jacob pulled out a fragmentation grenade and lobbed it over the compound wall. There was a shout, then a loud bang followed by screams.

"Cover me!" he told Jana as he rushed to the metal gate. It was a large set of twin doors made of thin metal, almost as high as the wall, in order to block the view inside. He pulled out a stun grenade and checked the gate.

Unlocked. Good. The soldiers thought they were the ones who were going to be attacking. They never figured they would end up having to defend the compound.

He pulled the pin, pushed the gate open a few inches, and tossed the stun grenade inside. Just as he dodged out of the way, a couple of bullets punctured the thin sheet metal just where he had been standing.

A moment later, there was a loud bang. Jacob unslung his assault rifle, but before he could get into the action, Jana kicked open the door and let out a three-round burst inside.

He rushed to join her.

The interior of the compound was typical for the region. A low concrete house stood in the center, a chicken coop and outhouse set to one side. Along the wall next to the road were stacked bales of hay that the soldiers had been standing on. Now those soldiers lay wounded or stunned, clutching their temporarily blinded eyes.

Jana let out another burst, taking out a guy's legs.

"Shoot them in the body!" Jacob shouted.

"They're not raiders." Jana fired again, hitting another man in the legs.

Jacob realized she was right. These guys were just provincial troops told they were lying in wait for foreign spies, which was actually true. They weren't thieves and killers preying on isolated villages.

Jacob spotted the front end of a Humvee poking out from the far side of the house. He ran that way and tossed another stun grenade around the corner. Once it went off, he rounded the corner and found two guys on their hands and knees, half unconscious. Two quick hits with the butt of his assault rifle made them fully unconscious.

In front of him was parked a Humvee and a troop transport truck. A three-round burst into the front tires of each meant they wouldn't have any pursuit.

Just as he finished this, the shutters of a window nearby opened. A young man in uniform pointed a rifle at him.

No choice. He took him out with a single shot. The man slumped over the window frame, blood leaking out of his skull.

You're a CIA assassin.

Little Mohammed's words came back to him, and he cringed.

There was movement inside the house—he tossed another stun grenade inside and sprinted back to Jana.

She had disabled every soldier and had taken up a position back outside the gate, using it to cover most of her body.

"Let's get out of here," he shouted as he ran for her. "I've disabled—"

A shot. Jacob felt a sharp pain and fell.

CHAPTER SEVENTEEN

Jana cried out as Jacob fell face-first into the dust. A soldier had risen up from the flat roof and shot him. Jana let out a burst, and the man ducked back down.

A moment later, he popped up on the other end of the roof, having rolled and gotten back into a firing position.

The bullet panged off the side of the metal gate, nearly taking off Jana's nose.

By the time she got to return fire, he had already ducked back down.

She spared a glance at Jacob. He lay motionless in the dirt, a dark stain spreading around him. Jana's entire body felt like it had been plunged into ice water.

Jana forced herself to look away and focus on the rooftop, trying to anticipate where the soldier would come up next.

She was off by a quarter of the width of the roof. She swiveled and fired in the same instant the soldier did.

His bullet hummed past her ear. Her bullet took him in the forehead.

She grimaced. She hadn't wanted to kill him, but she had no choice. For a moment, she looked at him slumped and lifeless, a young man following orders in a fight he didn't understand for hidden powers he had probably never heard of.

Jacob!

He still lay flat on the ground.

A quick glance to make sure there were no threats. Several soldiers lay on the ground, groaning and clutching their legs. None of them looked prepared to fight.

She bolted for Jacob. Just as she got to him, he sprang up, stumbled, gasped, and looked around.

"You're alive," Jana said. She couldn't believe it.

"I was playing dead because I didn't have cover. Thanks."

Now that she was closer, she could see a bullet had hit him in the fleshly part of the underarm. Blood soaked the left side of his body. He also had a big red mark on his forehead from faceplanting into the hard earth.

Jana felt a flare of irritation at him, not even trying to fight, which vanished instantly when he tried to get to the gate and staggered, having to hold himself up against the wall.

"Let's go," Jana said, supporting him on his uninjured side and leading him to the ravaged Land Rover. "Can you hold on long enough for me to drive a few miles away? I can't risk bandaging you up here."

"I've had worse," he said, falling more than sitting in the passenger's seat.

Jana got behind the wheel and sped off. All the farmers had vanished from the fields. She hunkered low and waited for more shots as she pulled away from the compound and got on the open road.

None came. If there were any soldiers in the area left uninjured, they were hiding.

Or radioing for help.

Their bullet-riddled Land Rover stuck out like a sore thumb. No way could they pass through a town or village without someone alerting the authorities.

She sped down the rough dirt track as fast as she dared, praying that the worn-out old tire wouldn't decide this was the perfect time to have a blowout. Jacob lay slumped against the side of the car, clutching his armpit and hissing with pain at each bounce.

"I'm sorry," he moaned.

"Don't worry. I'll patch you up."

"No, I mean I'm sorry about what happened back there."

"We were attacked. It wasn't your fault."

"You had to kill that guy. I know you didn't want to."

Gorge rose in her throat. She had been so hopped up on adrenaline that she hadn't had a chance to really absorb it. But yes, she had murdered someone. Well, forced by circumstances to murder someone. That didn't make it much better.

"I murdered someone too," Jacob whispered. His voice sounded weak. "Maybe Mohammed is right."

"You just hold on there."

Jana drove past the last of the farmhouses as the road descended to the desert. It looked like they had gotten away from the army for the moment, but now they were entering the open wasteland where bandits prowled. Perhaps the same ones they had defeated back at the village, the same ones burning for revenge.

She stopped the Land Rover a few miles after the last farmhouse. Grabbing the First Aid kit, she patched up Jacob. The bullet had gone right through the teres major muscle just below the left deltoid. Jacob wouldn't be using his left arm for a while.

She bandaged the wound, which had almost stopped bleeding already thanks to him keeping pressure on it the whole way and fashioned a sling for him. She was about to give him a tranquilizer, but he languidly shook his head.

"Got to stay alert," he murmured.

"You're in no shape for fighting."

"No tranquilizer."

"How do you feel?" she asked as she got back behind the wheel.

"Peachy. Get to a remote section of desert and we'll hide out until morning."

"All right."

Jana drove down the last of the foothills and sped off across a trackless section of the desert.

She made it five miles before the used tire gave out with a bang and a *flap flap flap* of flaccid rubber. She ground to a halt in the middle of a vast, searing plain.

"Huh?" Jacob said as she cursed a blue streak. From the sound of it, he had been sleeping.

"Never buy used tires."

"Sorry. I'll buy new ones the next time we're in rural Pakistan hiding from the government."

"You're going to be fine. Your dumb sense of humor has come back."

"To know me is to love me."

Jana got out and rounded the Land Rover with a sense of dread. Had the spare been shot up like last time?

She let out a great gust of relief to see that it hadn't. Not that there was much left of it. It was worn almost bald and had a faded look, like it had been left out to dry in the sun. Still, it was a tire.

They would have to drive slowly, avoiding any big ruts or sharp stones as much as possible, and hope they didn't have another blowout because Jacob was in no condition to walk to the nearest town, wherever the hell that was. And they couldn't go to the nearest town anyway because by now, the alert would have gone out, and every cop and every soldier in all of Balochistan would be on the lookout for them.

***

The campfire crackled, sending sparks up into the night sky. Jana fed another dry log onto it.

They were camped in a wadi, a dry riverbed she had driven the Land Rover into as the sun was setting. The high sides would keep the fire out of sight. Building a fire on the open plain would be suicide since it would act as a beacon for miles around.

Of course, camping in a wadi could be suicide too. A storm in the mountains miles away could send a torrent of water down the dry gulch powerful enough to sweep them and the Land Rover away. The famous nineteenth-century explorer and writer Isabel Eberhardt, a childhood heroine of Jana's, had died that way in Algeria. But Jana figured the risk of drowning in the desert was less than the risk of being spotted by bandits, so she had camped here.

Jacob lay with his back against a thick log, eyes hooded with weariness. She'd gotten some food and a bunch of water into him, and he looked better, at least better than the bloody mess back at the site of the ambush.

"You should get some sleep," Jana said.

"Got to finish the mission first."

"Tomorrow."

"Nope. Tonight. Go into the back of the Land Rover. In that secret compartment in the back Hashir showed us you'll find a metal case. Bring it to me."

Jana did as she was told, pulling out a heavy steel case about the size of a briefcase but thicker.

"What's this?" she asked, toting it over to him. He had sat up more and pulled out the thumb drive.

"A bulletproof laptop with a satellite phone."

"Can I buy one on Amazon?"

"Probably not, no."

She set it down for him, and because his left arm was still in a sling, she figured out the clasps and opened it for him. Inside the metal case was secured a laptop that was twice as thick as any regular one and made of durable steel. An old-style handset connected by a wire sat next to it.

He typed in a long password with his one good hand, and it showed a screen much like any other laptop, a detail that seemed odd to her.

She had figured it would be something special. The CIA logo or perhaps the eye in the pyramid.

Jacob inserted the thumb drive, and a folder came up. When he tried to open it, another password prompt stopped him. Again he typed in a long password.

"Amazing you can remember all these passwords. I'm always forgetting mine."

"No you're not. You're Aaron's daughter. Your mind is as sharp as his."

Jana chuckled. "I'm always saying self-defacing stuff like that to fit in."

"Well, you don't have to with me. You can be yourself."

Jana fell silent. After all of this chaos in her life, she wasn't sure what being herself even meant anymore.

The file folder opened to reveal several movie files. Jacob clicked on the most recent one from the day his colleagues got captured.

The video started with a shot of the excavation site slowly dwindling away as the drone gained altitude. A man holding a remote stood directly beneath it, looking up. He had a soldier's broad shoulders, hard body, and crew cut.

"Is that your friend?"

"Yeah," Jacob said, his voice heavy. "That's Robert."

The drone shot to the north and a little west, as shown in a readout on the lower right-hand corner. The readout also showed its altitude at five thousand feet and its speed at 300 mph.

300 mph? She didn't know drones could go that fast. Civilian drones probably couldn't. No wonder the local government got suspicious. Rugged mountains and thin strips of green valley passed below. Jacob fast-forwarded the video for a few minutes until he came to a point where the drone had stopped and was hovering.

"Bingo," he said.

The video showed a camp, three ragged rows of camouflage tents and stacks of crates nestled between two jagged ridges with a small stream passing through the middle. Off to one side were half a dozen Technicals and a bunch more Land Rovers and trucks. The camera zoomed in, focusing on the boxes. They looked strange to her, not like the usual crates one would put in the back of a truck.

Jacob let out a low whistle.

"This is worse than I thought. Way, way worse."

CHAPTER EIGHTEEN

Jacob realized that Robert and Oscar had hit the intel Mother Lode, and they nearly had missed getting that information out to the world.

The packing cases were made of lead. He could tell by its dull color and lack of reflection in the harsh mountain sun.

He also noticed a large tent nearby that all the militants seemed to avoid. For a few minutes, he and Jana watched the drone footage as the fighters swarmed over the rest of the camp, hurrying from one task to another but always making a point of giving the big tent a wide berth.

The drone hovered, using maximum magnification. Jacob could tell from the angle of the shadows that Robert had kept it between the sun and observers on the ground. That would make it invisible. While it would have been visible getting into position, the people on the ground, assuming they noticed it at all, would have seen it as a tiny speck high in the sky and would have probably mistaken it for a bird of prey or airplane.

Someone had spotted it, though.

But not before Robert and Oscar discovered something terrifying about this militia group.

After a minute, a white-suited figure waddled out of the tent. The drone descended a few hundred feet, the camera adjusting, the figure growing larger and clearer.

Jacob took in a sharp breath when the details came into view, and his worst suspicions were confirmed.

The guy was wearing a white Tyvek suit, black rubber gloves, and a face mask with a gas canister over the mouth.

Tyvek suits were used when handling radioactive substances.

The man picked up one of the lead cases and waddled back into the tent.

"Jesus," Jacob whispered. "They're making a dirty bomb."

"That's radioactive material in those cases?" Jana asked.

"Yeah. Stick a bunch of that in a conventional bomb and you can spread radiation across several city blocks. You can wreck a city for a decade, ruin the national economy for at least as long."

"My God, and the Balochi government is supporting this?"

"At least some elements. I bet most high officials don't even know what's going on. Most of the people in the provincial government aren't radicals, and even most radicals don't play with this sort of fire."

"Because the consequences are so harsh," Jana growled. "We have to stop them."

Jacob shook his head. "We don't have the strength. See how big that camp is? There's got to be a hundred, two hundred fighters there. Plus it's over several mountain passes that are probably guarded."

"We can't just leave them there! Which group is it?"

"I don't know. I'm sure previous intel has already identified the group. And it doesn't really matter. They got to be taken out whoever they are. I have to upload this to the satellite and let the high command decide. Hell, this will go straight to the president. I guess they'll advise him to call in an airstrike."

"The U.S. is going to launch an airstrike inside Pakistan?"

"It wouldn't be the first time. Washington will deny it, and the new Balochi leaders won't be able to complain without risking the U.S. revealing what they know. The Pakistani national government will no doubt be informed, and take our side. It will probably mean the end of Shia political power in Balochistan."

"But won't an airstrike spread radioactive material all over?"

Jacob nodded. "Afraid so. But they're in the middle of nowhere. Better there than Tehran or London."

Jana rubbed her temples. "Jesus. What a mess the world is."

"Big time. I got to set up the satellite dish. You go scout the perimeter. It would be just our luck to get surprised by bandits before I can upload the data."

Jana grabbed her gun and disappeared into the night, moving almost as quietly as a trained fighter. Aaron had brought her up well.

He thought of his old mentor as he unfolded the little satellite dish, an awkward task with only one hand, and used the computer to make the little motor in the tripod point it in the right location in the sky. Somewhere high above the earth, a chunk of metal and advanced electronics hung in geosynchronous orbit, ready to receive and retransmit data that would end hundreds of lives and save tens of thousands.

This is what Robert and Oscar had risked their lives for. And this is what Aaron had lost his life for—taking lives to save lives. It was a hell of a way to interact with the world. The curse of being important. But

Aaron hadn't hesitated to blow up that ISIS ammunition depot when it meant sacrificing his own life.

Or did he?

Had he really died?

He must have. Jacob couldn't see how he could have gotten out. And if he had, why the hell didn't Aaron hook up with him later?

Of course, he might have gotten away from the explosion and then gotten captured by ISIS fighters. His chances of surviving that, though, would have been less than sticking around and waiting for the munitions depot to go up. At least that would have been quick.

Plus, ISIS loved to publicize their tortures and beheadings. They couldn't have resisted showing off the brutal death of a CIA agent on every video platform.

The uplink connected, and Jacob had to put in a code to gain access to it. First, he sent the last video Robert and Oscar took. That was the most important one. At least, he thought so. There might be a whole lot of crap going on in those mountains. They sure took a lot of footage.

As the video uploaded, Jacob found himself still wondering about Aaron. Okay, if he hadn't lived, he would had shared his personal code with someone before the Raqqa mission, some trusted individual who knew almost immediately that Jana had been captured by The Order in Mexico City.

So why hadn't this guy revealed himself? Why didn't he help with the rescue effort since he was the one who launched it? Why the secrecy?

The first video was uploaded. He selected the rest of the videos in bulk and sent them on their way to orbit, where they would then be sent down to one or more of the field stations. He supposed both the field station in Islamabad and headquarters in Langley would take care of it. Wallace would check it out, too, in Athens since it was his operative who got sent into the line of fire. While the old soldier sent men and women into harm's way all the time, he always worried about them. The poor guy must have had a stomach full of ulcers.

So a bunch of high officials would put their heads together and decide what to do.

But what about him and Jana? Maybe they should make their way to Islamabad in case they were needed?

No. Karachi was much closer. Once he got there, he could use local CIA contacts to get further orders. He couldn't risk crossing the country with a bum shoulder and a civilian, no matter how kickass that civilian was.

He heard a small sound from outside the wadi and cocked his ear, reaching for his assault rifle before realizing he couldn't use it one-handed.

The sound repeated.

Casting a last glance at the computer to check that it was still uploading, he slipped into a shadowy spot behind a cluster of bushes. There he hunkered down, drew his pistol, and waited.

For a moment, he heard no sound. He cast nervous glances at his computer, so vital to the operation, sitting vulnerable and in plain sight. What if someone realized its importance and put a bullet through it? At least he got the most important video uploaded. Hopefully, that would be enough.

Another soft sound, as of someone coming down the steep side of the wadi several yards outside the range of the firelight and accidentally loosening a bit of sand.

Where was Jana? Had she heard this too? Jacob watched the shadows, waiting for one of them to move.

Then he saw a figure moving down the wadi, walking right down the center in full view. He aimed at it, then let out a breath of relief when he saw Jana walk into the light.

Jana saw the camp abandoned, and the look on her face touched something in him.

It wasn't fear, although there was some of that too. No, it was mostly worrying for him.

Him. Jacob Snow.

How many other people showed true worry about him? Sure, his boss, but it was his boss who sent him into danger in the first place.

"Psst."

Jana went prone and pointed her gun in his direction.

"It's me," Jacob whispered. "Is everything all right?"

He felt almost bad to see that look of worry disappear from her face.

"Yeah. Everything good here?"

Jacob stood and walked into the light. "Yeah. We just spooked each other. It happens."

"I did a circuit of the camp and didn't see anything."

"Good." Jacob strolled over to the laptop and little satellite dish, feeling buoyant at the memory of that look. It made the pain in his side and the bigger pain in his shoulder worth it.

The files had been uploaded.

"Phew! Mission accomplished." He turned off the computer and shut the case. "I think I'll sleep for ten hours, and then we'll make our way back to Karachi. We'll have to ditch this vehicle and get another. We have enough cash for some cheap jalopy."

Jana stared at him, confusion drawing out her features. "Wait. We're leaving?"

"Yeah." Jacob gestured at the laptop. "Mission accomplished."

"What about Robert and Oscar?"

Jacob grimaced, his shoulders slumping. "We can't bust them out. I'm wounded."

"We can't just leave them there. They'll be tortured to death."

"Washington is trying diplomacy," Jacob said, not convincing himself.

He didn't convince Jana either.

"Diplomacy isn't going to work, or if it does they might be too late. They'll torture those guys to get more information out of them, something they can use as leverage. The provincial government must know they're walking on the razor's edge, and they know they don't have much time. They'll *need* to torture them."

"They wouldn't dare torture American citizens."

Jana hunkered down next to the fire, the crackling flames casting a garish glow over her face. "In a normal situation, no, but this isn't a normal situation. The new Balochi government knows the central government wants to crush them, and now that they've caught a couple of American spies, the Americans want to crush them too. But they don't have proof they're spies. They need to get that. It's they're only way to survive. Then they can show themselves to be patriotic heroes, stopping foreign meddling in Pakistan. That would make them look great while seriously embarrassing the central government."

Jacob stared into the flames. She was right. In his heart, he had known it all along, although he couldn't face it. Robert, a comrade-in-arms from a long time back, suffering in some horrible prison. And Oscar, too, another good man.

"It's impossible," he murmured.

"Do you know where they're being held?"

Jacob nodded, still looking into the flames.

"Is it far?"

"No, just a couple of hours."

"We could go now."

"Not at night. The road there is closed at night."

"So we go tomorrow?"

"And do what? We're out of frag grenades. I can't use anything but a pistol."

"I'm uninjured except for that graze on my arm. That stings but doesn't affect my movement at all."

Jacob looked up at her. "Jana, this is a prison, staffed by soldiers. Getting them out would require a team of SEALS or Rangers."

"Which our government isn't going to send," Jana replied.

"Because they don't want the situation blowing up in their faces, which is exactly what will happen if we go."

Jana looked him in the eye. "So we leave two men behind."

Jacob cringed. That had been her father speaking. That had been his own conscience speaking. In the Rangers, his old outfit, they had a policy of never leaving a man behind, no matter what the cost. The Navy SEALs possessed the same ideal. All the elite units did.

Jacob looked back into the fire, looking into his future. He saw himself following orders and returning home without Robert Murphy and Oscar Dortmund. He saw himself trying to rationalize it and failing. He saw a little seed of self-hatred being planted in his heart and beginning to grow.

No. He had enough of that already.

He began to set up the satellite antenna again as an idea formed in his mind and the beginnings of a plan.

CHAPTER NINETEEN

When Jacob got his boss, Athens Station Director Tyler Wallace, on the satellite phone, the old soldier sounded both relieved and confused.

"I can confirm that the intel has made it to us, Agent Snow. You should have gotten a confirmation in return. Did the satellite not do that?"

"It did, but I have something else to talk to you about."

"What's that?"

"I wanted to ask if there was any plan to bust out Agents Murphy and Dortmund."

Wallace paused. Jacob could hear a sigh come over the satellite connection. Jacob glanced around the dark beyond the campfire. Jana had gone out on patrol again.

"There is no plan at this time."

Jacob rubbed his temples. Now he had no choice. No choice he could live with, anyway.

"I'm just two hours away. I can see what I can do."

"Jacob, you're alone. You can't break into that prison."

Jacob winced. He'd be in deep trouble if Wallace knew that he actually wasn't alone.

"I've done similar operations before solo."

When I had two good arms and a lot of prep work.

"It's too risky. You don't have backup. We don't have a plan to extract you."

"They're probably getting tortured in there. The Balochis haven't found any hard evidence of spying. They need to get that from them or their position becomes untenable."

"I know, I know." Wallace's voice sounded grim. It also carried a note of expectancy. He knew where this conversation was heading. He knew his star agent all too well.

"I have to try, sir."

"I can't authorize that."

"I'm not asking you to."

Silence. It seemed to stretch out for hours, although it probably only lasted a couple of seconds.

"There will be hell to pay. Not from me, but from Washington."

"I've saved the world for them how many times?"

"That's not how they think and you know it."

"I have to try," Jacob repeated.

"I know, Agent Snow." His tone had become indulgent, almost fatherly.

Jacob paused, imagining the fallout of this all went south, which it probably would: him dead or captured, Wallace stripped of his rank and drummed out of service. Tyler Wallace, one of the best men in the CIA.

His boss knew the consequences as much as he did, and yet he was still willing to go through with it.

Jacob's respect for him, already great, rose to an even higher level.

"Can you send me the latest satellite images of the prison?"

"Sure. It's a small prison, so while we don't know where exactly they're being held, they shouldn't be too hard to find if you manage to infiltrate the place."

"What kind of protection is there?"

"The usual high concrete wall topped with razor wire and guard towers. A supply truck enters at roughly nine every morning. Other vehicles at irregular hours, sometimes after dark. There doesn't seem to be any lockdown time."

"That's a plus," Jacob said, checking his watch. It wasn't even ten P.M. yet.

"No heavy ordinance or armor," Wallace said. "A couple of armored personnel carriers are parked inside, plus an armored prisoner bus. No mortars or heavy machine guns or anything like that. I'm sure the guards are armed well enough, though, and don't assume they're the usual second-rank soldiers put on easy guard duty. Given who they're guarding, they'll have been backed up with top soldiers."

"Great. Any idea of garrison size?"

"At least thirty. Maybe as many as fifty. Not including checkpoints on the roads and the garrison in a nearby town fifteen miles away. That garrison is at least another fifty."

"So thirty to one are my best odds, and a hundred and thirty to one are my worst."

"Plus the troops at the checkpoints."

"Right," Jacob said, rubbing his eyes. "Can't forget to invite them to the party."

“You don’t have to do this.”

“Yeah I do.”

“I know, Agent Snow.”

“Can you send me the latest images? I need to get to work on this.”

“I’m sending them along right now.”

“Thanks.”

“Best of luck, Agent Snow. Let’s hope the higher-ups don’t hang us for this.”

“I appreciate you going out on the limb for me.”

“I’m going out on a limb for those two agents.”

“Right. Thanks anyway, sir.”

A series of satellite images appeared in the download folder. Jacob opened them and began to study.

He was already deep into thought when Jana came back a couple of minutes later.

“Did he say yes?”

“Well, he didn’t say no,” Jacob said, indicating the satellite images.

Jana sat cross-legged beside him and studied the one he had up at the moment, a wide view of the area. The prison—an ugly rectangle of concrete—stood in a dry little valley surrounded by low mountains. Fifteen miles to the southwest was a town of about five thousand people, a fort clearly visible alongside the main road that led south to more populated areas. A few villages were scattered around the countryside, dotting the narrow valleys fed by mountain streams. None were close.

A paved road led from the town to the prison. There were also two dirt roads, one from the north and the other from the east.

Getting to the north one would require a long detour over rough terrain. The eastern road was better but passed through two villages before approaching the valley where the prison stood. A mile before the road humped over a ridge and descended into the valley stood a roadblock just outside the second village.

The roadblock didn’t look very big, a few guys at most, but it was bound the have a radio to communicate with the prison.

Could the radio even reach the prison? There was a mountain between them. He bet they had put a repeater on top of the mountain to receive the signal from one side and send it on to another.

He zoomed in on the mountaintop and looked. Sure enough, he spotted a square base of concrete about a yard to the side, the gleam of metal in the sunlight, and the faintest thin shadow.

Yep, they had a repeater up there because that's what made sense. The Balochis weren't stupid. Well, their politicians might be, but not their local armed forces.

Just his luck.

We're going to get killed.

Well, I probably will be. Not Jana. I can't let that happen to Jana.

After a moment, Jacob said, "Here's what I think. We hit the place now, as soon as we can. It will take about three hours from our current position to get to this checkpoint here. You drive so I can rest. Not sure I can handle a stick shift anyway. With any luck, we won't run across any bandits or patrols until we get to this checkpoint."

"And then what?" Jana asked.

Jacob smiled. "And then we give them a little surprise."

***

Their luck had held, and Jacob had managed to get more than two hours of sleep in the passenger's seat before Jana roused him. He snapped awake instantly.

He whisked away the cloth that he had used to shield himself from the sand streaming in from the wrecked windshield. A good thing he had that too because his hands, arms, hair, and chest were covered in a fine coating of it. Poor Jana must have spit out half a desert.

He saw from the headlights that they had left the lowland desert behind and were driving along a winding mountain road, a steep hill to one side and not a sign of life anywhere.

"We just passed the first village," Jana told him. "The second one is coming up."

"Good. No trouble on the road?"

"You slept the whole way, didn't you?" she asked with a smile in her voice.

"You might have kicked ass so efficiently and silently that I didn't wake up."

"Very flattering. How do you feel?"

"As rested as I can be. My right arm feels a bit better but I still can't use it for anything."

"With your plan, hopefully we won't have to."

The second village came into sight, a collection of low stone buildings with slate roofs. At this hour, not a single light was on. Good. No one to see their passing.

He readied a flash grenade and squirmed down in his seat. When Jana took the Land Rover around a broad curve, and they spotted a light up ahead, he squirmed down even lower.

A white boom was set across the road. To the left of it and a little behind stood a small concrete guardhouse. In front of it stood a couple of thick steel shields five feet high with firing slits, one-man protection used by sentries all over the Middle East.

A guard stood behind one of them. Another stood in the open on the other side of the road, wearing a bulletproof vest and helmet, shielding his face from the glare of the high beams Jana had deliberately switched on. A couple more walked out of the concrete building to the left of the road.

The guy with his hand in front of his face shouted something, no doubt an angry command to stop blinding him.

"Ready?" Jana whispered.

"Sure." Jacob got out of sight below the dashboard.

Jana came to a stop just in front of the boom and stepped out. There was the sound of boots crunching gritty soil. Jana reached back into the Land Rover and turned off the headlights. A spotlight came on, lighting her up.

Cries of surprise from the guards at seeing a lone foreign woman in the middle of nowhere in the middle of the night.

Then a barked question. They'd spotted the bullet holes.

"Oh, those?" Jana asked in a cheerful voice. "Those are just a little decoration I added. And why bother with windows? I like to breathe the fresh air."

The footsteps came closer, accompanied by another rough question.

"Looks like they're all here," Jana said in the same tone of voice as before.

Jacob pulled the pin from his flash grenade and lobbed it over the dashboard. He had a brief glimpse of five men. The guy behind the shield gaping at the foreign woman, the guy to the right of the road grinning like he hadn't seen a woman in weeks, which he probably hadn't, two more men advancing from the building flanking an officer who gave the unexpected foreigner a suspicious scowl.

All of them turned at the metallic clunk of the grenade bouncing off the Land Rover's hood.

Jacob ducked back down, closing his eyes and putting his fingers in his ears. Jana dove back into the Land Rover and did the same.

A loud bang and flash of light nearly overwhelmed his senses despite taking cover and taking precautions. Jacob shook himself and leaped out of the Land Rover.

Jana was way ahead of him. She rushed right into the crowd of guys, all lying or kneeling on the ground, stunned and blinded. She managed to bind the wrists of the two nearest soldiers with zip cuffs before the other three began to show signs of waking up, meaning they were staggering around, blinking their eyes and trying to figure out what to aim at.

Dangerous enough. Drawing his pistol, Jacob rushed for the nearest one. Just as the man blearily looked in his direction, trying to focus, Jacob pistol-whipped him.

He dropped like a sack of oats. The second one turned, leveling his assault rifle, sensing but not fully seeing danger. Jacob knocked his gun aside and kicked the guy's legs out from under him.

The soldier landed hard, then lay still after Jacob pistol-whipped him too.

A shot rang out. The officer had fired, but in his mostly blinded state, the bullet went wide.

Another shot rang out, and the officer let out a cry, and he fell, a bullet through the fleshy part of his thigh.

"Damn it!" Jana said. "I wanted to avoid that."

"His fault for being tough." Jacob walked over to the writhing officer, kicked the pistol out of his hand, and zip-cuffed him. Then he checked the building, found a radio he had trashed, then made a quick circuit of the area. No one else in sight.

A Hummer sat behind the building with the keys in the ignition, just as he had hoped.

That village was just a couple of miles down the road, though. Somebody would probably come to investigate the gunshots soon.

Jacob moved back to the officer, plucked the beret off his head and put it on himself. Not much of a disguise, but if they saw him in silhouette or in the near darkness, they might be fooled for a crucial second or two.

"You find any grenades?" he called over to Jana.

"No."

"Damn. That would have been nice. I found a Hummer. Let's get all the gear loaded into it."

That took just a minute. Then Jacob pointed to one of the half-conscious figures trussed up with zip cuffs. The guy was young and thin, sporting a mustache that he probably only got to fully grow in the past couple of years.

"He looks the most pliable. Put him in the front passenger's seat."

Jana did as she was asked. As she dragged the limp form out of sight behind the guardhouse, Jacob hurried back to the Land Rover, drew his knife, and slashed two of the tires; then, he ran back to the Hummer just as Jana was finishing.

He got into the driver's seat.

"You're going to drive one-handed?" Jana asked.

"I can kinda sorta use my bad hand as long as I don't move my shoulder too much. I need you to fire and take care of Sleeping Beauty here."

"All right," Jana said, moving to get into the back.

"Wait, could you just go and check the road to the village for a minute?"

"Will do."

Jana ran back around the guardhouse.

As soon as she got out of sight, Jacob turned on the ignition, got the Hummer into gear, wincing at the pain that caused his wounded shoulder, and sped off down the road toward the prison.

CHAPTER TWENTY

Jana swore and spat as she ran after the Hummer, enveloped in a cloud of dust. After a few yards, she stopped, the Hummer's lights dwindling into the distance.

Jacob had left her again, deciding that she was too weak and precious to go on this mission and thinking he could do it all alone, and wounded at that! Idiot. Did he think she was much safer here, hanging out at an army checkpoint with a bunch of half-conscious soldiers and a village that was bound to investigate the shots in the next few minutes?

She ran back to the Land Rover, hopped in, and got the vehicle started.

"You forgot I have a vehicle too," she growled under her breath. She popped the Land Rover into gear and moved forward, only to hear the *slap slap slap* of a dead tire. She punched the steering wheel.

"Damn it!"

She got out and looked at the flat. No, two flats.

"Idiot! A complete, utter idiot! What am I supposed to do, just hang out in the mountains until he decides to come back for me?"

The whine of an underpowered motorcycle cut through the night air. Jana whipped around and saw a headlight in the distance, rapidly approaching.

She lay face down in the dirt near one of the unconscious soldiers, her face toward the motorcycle, eyes narrowed to slits. The motorcycle stopped about a hundred yards away and switched off, plunging the dirt road into darkness. The scene of the fight was fully lit, however. Jana included.

"Mohammed!" someone called.

Probably the officer's name.

"Mohammed!" the voice called again.

With the light shining from the guardhouse, whoever was on the motorcycle could clearly see the ravaged Land Rover and the bodies lying all around. A couple of the soldiers shifted and groaned, slowly coming out of it.

The sound of movement. Two figures emerged from the darkness, one a policeman and one a civilian, who had probably had his bike commandeered for an unwelcome late-night excursion.

The policeman had his assault rifle leveled. The civilian hung back.

They both paused about twenty yards from the scene. The cop called out something in Balochi. One of the soldiers lying near Jana moaned out a response. She could hear him shifting his weight.

The cop rushed over to him and just past Jana. She lashed out, kicking him in the back of the knee. The guy fell, and Jana rose, slamming the butt of her assault rifle into his forehead and knocking him out cold.

The civilian squawked and ran off into the night, looking like a panicked ghost in his white jalwar kemeez. He headed for his motorbike. A shot fired well over his head made him veer off into the hills.

Jana ran over to the bike, found the keys still in the ignition, slung her assault rifle over her back, and revved it up. She paused for a moment. That villager had looked pretty poor. This motorbike was probably his family's pride and joy, maybe even their means to make a living. Reaching into her pocket, she pulled out a wad of local currency. She didn't even bother to count it. She just gave him the whole thing. Chances were, she wouldn't need money at all after tonight.

She set it under a stone in the middle of the road and sped off, driving past the wrecked Land Rover, past the moaning soldiers, and off into the dark night of rural Pakistan.

She hoped she could remember the way to the prison from their study of the terrain back at camp. She hoped she'd get there before Jacob got into more trouble than he could handle. Most of all, she hoped she'd still find him alive.

***

The soldier had been cursing Jacob steadily and without a break for the past half hour in both Balochi and Urdu.

Since Jacob knew neither language, it didn't really bother him. Besides, the poor guy had every right to be angry. He'd been hit with a flash bang, pistol-whipped, and woke up to find himself with his hands zip-cuffed behind his back, a prisoner in his own unit's Hummer, and his captor didn't even understand his insults. Jacob figured he kept on with the profanity as a coping mechanism.

The road began to descend into a valley of utter darkness. He remembered from the satellite images that there were no villages here, nothing except the prison itself. It should be coming into sight soon. He hoped. He didn't dare stop and look at his computer again. No time. Who knew what might be coming on the road chasing him?

He felt a tremor of worry over Jana. He had ditched her there in the middle of nowhere with a heap of incriminating evidence and no way to get away from the villagers who would be sure to come to investigate.

She had some good sense, though. All she had to do was bug out into the hills and hide until he got back. If he got back. If he didn't, she'd be in deep trouble.

Less trouble than if she came along. Breaking into this prison was one of the longest longshots he'd ever tried—break into a prison alone with inadequate intel to spring a couple of operatives, and all with an arm that was giving him more and more pain? He'd ground the gears more than once, already trying to shift and not being able to put enough strength and coordination into moving the stick.

He rounded a hairpin turn and saw lights glimmering down on the valley floor. The prison stood out as a stark concrete rectangle, with towers on each corner, floodlights shining a harsh white light on the desiccated plain all around.

Jacob brought the Hummer to a halt. He got out, listened for the sounds of approaching motors and, hearing none, opened the passenger's side door and pointed a pistol at the prisoner, gesturing for him to get out.

The man started praying one of the *shahada*, the Muslim declaration of faith, which Muslims the world over use as a standard prayer.

"Relax," Jacob said in what he hoped was a reassuring voice. A difficult thing to do when you're pointing a gun at someone.

The man got out, took a deep breath and stood up straight. He kept praying.

Jacob gestured for him to lie face down. The man got to his knees, looked for one longing moment at the starry sky, then got in the dirt, praying louder.

Jacob holstered his pistol, drew his knife, and cut the zip cuff restraining his wrists.

The soldier stopped praying and dared a peek over his shoulder. Jacob smiled at him, sheathed his knife, and drew his pistol again. Then he gestured for the man to get up. He did so, looking at Jacob curiously, a glimmer of hope in his young eyes. Jacob gestured for him to get behind the steering wheel.

The penny dropped. The soldier looked to the prison and back at Jacob again and hesitated.

Jacob pressed the gun to the man's temple, hoping the guy didn't call his bluff.

The man's eyes flicked in the direction of the prison again, then slumped his shoulders a little.

Too much. It was a show. Jacob could tell from the calculating look in the guy's eyes. He was going to play along, wait for a chance, and try something.

Fair enough. That's what Jacob would do in his situation. And he didn't really have a choice except to use this guy as cover to get into the prison. No hope of finishing the mission otherwise.

And yes, the mission wasn't finished until he got Robert Murphy and Oscar Dortmund safely home.

The soldier got behind the wheel, watching Jacob with a wary eye. His gaze kept going to Jacob's injured arm. A spot of blood had seeped through the bandage. With a wound like this, he should really be laid up in the hospital and not moving it at all.

No choice. Jacob gestured with his pistol, and the young soldier put the Hummer into drive and began to move down the winding mountain road.

Through those last long miles, Jacob kept his eye on the driver while trying to note everything around him. He saw no lights from other vehicles or even any distant villages or farmhouses. It seemed the Balochis wanted their prison as isolated as possible. Even if a prisoner busted out, there wouldn't be anywhere for a man to get to on foot.

They got to the plain, and the driver picked up some speed, getting on a well-worn dirt track. He didn't even need to ask where Jacob wanted to go.

The prison loomed up before them. Jacob, knowing he was invisible behind the windshield and the glare of the headlights, stayed put and studied the situation.

On each corner stood guard towers manned by two men each. A large metal gate was closed. Next to it was a small window, no doubt of bulletproof glass and too small for a man to fit through.

The soldier pulled to a halt in front of the gate. Jacob jabbed his pistol into his ribs. After an uncertain look at Jacob, who glared back at him, he rolled down the window and shouted something in Balochi. Jacob prayed he wasn't revealing anything like Jana had done when they pulled their little trick back at the roadblock. If he was smart and kept his head together, that's exactly what he'd do.

Jacob would just have to hope that this guy was like most people and couldn't think clearly with a gun shoved into his side.

Pause. No answer from the gate or the guard towers. Jacob gave the guy a nudge. He shouted out something else.

Why the hell did I get this assignment when I don't speak any of the local languages? He could be calling in an airstrike, for all I know.

There was a loud clang and the gates started to creak open on electric-powered gears. They revealed a long, low concrete building with no windows about thirty yards beyond, no doubt the prisoners' housing. To one side was an exercise yard with a wire fence topped with razor wire. To the left stood a barracks. A couple of bored-looking soldiers sauntered to the entrance and stood there as Jacob's captive drove toward the gate.

Jacob cursed and reached past him to raise the window. Then he leaned back and hoped the beret he wore would be enough of a disguise. Just as the Hummer passed by the guard on Jacob's side, he leaned forward as if searching for something at his feet.

When he raised up a moment later, he saw the guard he had been hiding from press a button to close the gate again. Jacob nudged his prisoner and pointed to a spot beyond the barracks where several vehicles were parked. Compared with the rest of the compound, it was poorly lit.

They drove there, passing no one at this late hour, Jacob wondering all the while what the guy had told the guards at the gate. So far, he had seen no signs of trouble or increased alertness.

Just as they were parking, he saw the prisoner's hand ease toward the door. A jab with the pistol stopped that movement.

They parked. The young soldier turned to him, meeting his eye in the half-light. Where before Jacob had seen fear and craftiness, now he saw only steel.

The soldier hit the horn and held it. A loud blare echoed around the compound, slapping off the concrete walls to redouble in volume. Jacob pistol-whipped him. The man's hand fell off the horn, his body sinking into unconsciousness and slumping down in the seat.

“Sleep well, soldier,” Jacob said, a note of admiration in his voice.

He leaped out of the Hummer and bolted for the shadows behind the barracks, hoping and praying he wouldn’t be spotted, that no one would look at the strange sound of a visiting soldier hitting his horn right by the barracks after midnight. Fat chance. There was a shout from the nearest tower and a shouted reply from the gate, followed quickly by the sound of running footsteps.

CHAPTER TWENTY ONE

Jacob glanced around, knowing he had little cover and that he needed to make a move now. They had spotted him from one of the towers, a man dressed in civilian, Western clothing hopping out of an army Hummer. A sight that was beyond suspicious.

He had found a blind spot behind the barracks between an electric generator and a foul-smelling garbage bin. There were no other blind spots he could see nearby, no door into the barracks on this side of the building, and no time to hide himself further.

Besides, the guards knew every inch of this place. He had to get to Robert and Oscar now, spring them, grab some weapons, and maybe the three of them together could blast their way out.

The prison block stood not far from the barracks, across twenty yards of open dirt. He had seen a single steel door at the front on his way in. Nothing more.

Gripping his pistol, he ran for it.

And came under fire almost immediately.

Someone on the nearest guard tower opened up with an assault rifle, the bullets stitching a line in the dirt just behind him. The two guys at the front gate were running toward him, and as he burst out into the open, they both dropped to one knee and aimed.

Jacob fired at them, a tough shot at medium range while running and using only a 9mm pistol.

His first shot took out one anyway. That made the other throw himself in the dirt. Jacob fired again, wasn't sure if he hit or not, and then had to zigzag as the guy in the tower kept firing.

He was almost to the door. If it was locked, he'd be screwed. He might be able to shoot off the lock before he got hit, but if it was bolted from the inside, it wouldn't matter.

And now that he was dead center of the compound, a second tower opened up on him. Bullets spat up dirt all around him or cracked off the concrete surface of the wall.

But every now and then in battle, when the situation looks hopeless, the enemy gives you a gift.

That gift came in the form of a very stupid prison guard.

A big hulking guy with a Neanderthal forehead, unibrow over beady eyes, and an assault rifle that looked tiny in his massive paws actually opened the door and barreled out, perhaps thinking he'd blow away this foreigner like Rambo and get that promotion that had always passed him by. Jacob imagined him beating prisoners while looking at his superior officer with a hopeful grin like a dog performing a trick and seeking approval.

Jacob parted that unibrow with a bullet and rushed inside.

Only to find himself in an antechamber with no exit except another steel door.

He tried it. Locked, of course.

Probably not by Unibrow but by a slightly more intelligent guard on the other end of that security camera that pointed right at him.

Jacob gave the camera the finger, then shot at the lock.

The bullet took out the lock, then ricocheted around two walls before flying out the open door.

Jacob flinched and swore, then put his good shoulder against the steel door. It rattled in its frame, getting stopped after a fraction of an inch by a bolt on the other side.

Great. Just great.

He ran to the open door and immediately had to duck back in the brunt of heavy crossfire from the two front watchtowers. The building had been placed so that any prisoner who managed to get to the front door could be cut down in an instant.

Another burst of fire brought a couple of bullets through the open doorway to bang around the inside of the small room. Jacob cursed and pulled the steel door shut, but not before he saw half a dozen guards advancing on his position.

Using the door as a shield, he opened it a crack and fired out, taking down one of the advancing guards. A rattle of automatic fire came as a response, clanging off the steel door.

Jacob spared a look over his shoulder. The other door, leading further inside the prison, remained securely shut. But for how long? They were probably massing a group to burst through there at any moment to gun him down, and he would have nowhere to run or hide.

The firing tapered off. There was a screech of feedback as a loudspeaker somewhere out in the yard came on.

Someone shouted a command in Urdu. There was a pause, a muttered conversation, then a new voice came on.

This one spoke English.

"You are surrounded. There is no hope for escape. Surrender now and we will spare your life."

Jacob fired a round at the guards. He only managed to graze one, but it communicated what he thought of that proposal.

Another burst of fire hammered on the steel door. After the firing died down, the voice continued.

"We know you have come here to try and release the two spies. You have failed. Surrender now or we will kill one of them. We do not need both."

Jacob paused.

"Throw your weapons out the door and come out with your hands up. You have to the count of ten before I give the order to kill one of the prisoners. One … "

Jacob slumped. He had no choice. They would be good to their word and kill either Robert or Oscar. They didn't need both.

What an idiot you are. You think you're Superman? You've only made the situation worse.

"Two … "

He tossed his pistol out, then his knife. Slowly he opened the door, raising his good hand far above his head and painfully trying to get his injured arm to extend enough.

The guards rushed toward him, guns leveled.

The loudspeaker blared again. "You are now a prisoner of the Balochi government. If you resist, you and your companions will die."

***

"You are now a prisoner of the Balochi government. If you resist, you and your companions will die."

Jana's heart pounded in her chest when she heard the loudspeaker say that.

Lying prone in the dark desert a hundred yards beyond the reach of the floodlights, she had heard the gun battle and the commands from the prison guards. She listened as the prison descended into silence, hoping for more gunshots, anything that would indicate that Jacob had pulled a trick and was fighting his way out.

There was nothing.

Jana crawled back for a few hundred yards, then got up and jogged back to where she had parked the motorcycle at the point where the mountain road made it to the valley. It had been a crazy drive down that winding, rocky road with the lights off, and now she would have to make that journey back up again. They'd be sure to send out patrols to look for Jacob's backup.

And she'd be his backup. No way would she leave him stuck in there. The question was—how the hell to get in? Sneaking in under cover of a military vehicle had been a good idea, but that hadn't worked, and they'd be twice as vigilant now. She'd have to find another way. But what other way? She had no idea. She had only one hope she could think of, and that meant running right back to the danger she had fled a few hours before. Because hidden in a secret compartment in the Land Rover was the laptop and satellite phone. Jacob had left it behind, not wanting to risk having it fall into the hands of the enemy, and Jana had made the same decision. Assuming she could get back to the Land Rover and assuming she could avoid the seriously pissed-off guys at the checkpoint, she might be able to put in a call for backup.

Even though she didn't know the password. Well, she'd have to cross that bridge when she came to it. The shortwave transceiver was in the same hidden compartment. Maybe she could put out a distress call on that, although to who she had no idea.

As she drove up the mountain road, peering at the rough track ahead lit only by starlight, something niggled at the back of her mind. The shortwave transceiver. Something about that. Did she know anyone she could send a message to? No, that wasn't quite it. But it was something to do with the shortwave radio band.

Suddenly it hit her. She stopped the motorcycle, turned on the flashlight on her phone, and pulled out the business card for the fake Pakistani taxi service with phone numbers that didn't exist in any known country.

She studied the numbers, which had bothered her all this long trip.

There were three.

"202 007 121
212 014 121
132 028 121"

"When you're looking at something you don't understand, look for patterns. That's the key to unlock the answer."

That's what Dad always said.

First off, all three "phone numbers" ended in 121. Plus, the third and fourth numbers were 20.

Could it be for a 24-hour clock? 2020, 2120, 1320.

If so, that left the other numbers. 07121, 14121, 28121.

Then it hit her. Those could be frequencies in the shortwave band. 7.121 MHz, 14.121 MHz, and 28.121 MHz. Dad had an shortwave amateur radio at home, and she recalled those frequencies fell in the amateur "ham radio" band.

So could these be times and frequencies to call?

Call who?

Her heart trembled at the possibilities.

Now she needed to get back to the Land Rover more than ever.

Revving up her motorcycle, she headed back up the mountain pass, heading away from Jacob and in the only direction she could go that might save him.

***

Jacob was marched down a bare concrete hallway, his hands cuffed behind his back and his wounded shoulder in so much pain he didn't even feel the black eye and bruised ribs they'd given him after he had surrendered.

The guards led him through a large room with a medical table in the middle splashed with blood and a system of restraints on the wall and ceiling. A shelf to one side held various whips, electric prods, and dental tools.

"You'll be coming here soon," said an officer in English. Then he said something in Balochi, and the three guards escorting him laughed.

They came to a corridor lined with cell doors. One of the guards opened one with a heavy brass key. Another removed the handcuffs, while the third kept a gun pointed at his head. The officer shoved him so hard that Jacob slammed into the back wall of the cell and collapsed in agony.

"Enjoy your stay. We will see you soon."

They slammed the door shut and locked it with a loud click.

Jacob sat up and paused for a moment, easing his arm back into position. The bandage was soaked with blood now. He put his free hand against it and put as much direct pressure on the wound as he could bear.

He found himself in a ten-foot by ten-foot concrete cell lit by a single bare bulb in a steel bracket. An army sleeping bag in the corner was the only furniture unless one counted the stinking hole of a toilet.

The door had a peephole in the middle and a slit on the floor to pass food through.

Someone called out in Urdu from another cell.

"You speak Arabic?" Jacob called back.

"Yes. Who are you?"

"No one who's going to live through the night," Jacob said.

"What happened? The guards were shouting that there was an attack on the prison."

The voice sounded familiar, even through the filter of a foreign language.

"Are you one of the spies?" Jacob asked.

Pause. "Wait. They spoke to you in English."

Jacob decided to risk it. "Remember Chiapas?"

He figured if this was a plant, some locals wouldn't even know where Chiapas was.

"Jacob!"

"Robert! How are you?"

"Locked up in here. They haven't tortured me. They tortured our foreman, poor guy, and Oscar too. They're both unconscious in their cells."

Jacob's mind raced. They were probably being recorded, so they had to speak without saying anything directly.

"I heard that was a very fruitful excavation," Jacob said. "The initial results are already getting published."

"Oh my God, I can't tell you how happy that makes me." Robert sounded like someone who had just found out his wife had made it through life-or-death surgery.

Of course, he didn't have a wife. Neither did Oscar. Neither did Jacob. They were all single men. Perpetually single men.

Jacob shoved that unwelcome, intrusive thought aside and asked, "I don't suppose you've found a way out of here?"

"No, I'm surprised you found a way in."

"Not very far in. I'm disabled in one arm, and there's no one else coming."

I hope Jana doesn't try. No way she'd get past the gate. Trying it would be suicide. Just like I've committed suicide. A slow suicide by torture. They'll come for me, sooner rather than later.

CHAPTER TWENTY TWO

Jana ditched the bike a mile down the road from where she estimated the checkpoint to be, hoping its high-pitched whine hadn't carried that far in the cold mountain air. Leaving it out of sight from the road in case she had to come back to it, she tromped up the rough dirt track that had given her so much trouble on that cheap motorcycle, assault rifle at the ready, eyes and ears alert.

The road seemed abandoned. No vehicles had passed. Why hadn't they gone down to the prison to check on it? Maybe they were on strict instructions to remain at their post no matter what.

As she walked, she turned over those fake telephone numbers in her mind. Yes, it made sense. Times and frequencies. The question was, were those local times or UTC? Radio operators tended to use Universal Time Coordinated because it was global, set to an hour behind Greenwich Mean Time and a constant for everyone. That way, if a radio operator gave a certain time to get back in touch with someone in another country, there would be no confusion.

So yes, probably UTC. She'd try both UTC and local time, just in case.

Assuming she could overpower the guards, get the radio, and set it up somewhere.

Big, big assumption.

She rounded another hairpin turn and saw a light in the road up ahead. She stopped, ready to dive behind a nearby boulder, but then saw it wasn't moving.

Approaching with caution, she began to make out details. A concrete building. The gleam of light off the metal of a couple of vehicles.

The army checkpoint.

She moved off the road into rougher terrain that would hopefully act as cover and approached with care. As she got within a few hundred yards, still well beyond the shine of the light, she could see figures walking around.

Jana got low and moved as quietly as she could. The Land Rover still stood where they had left it. Two Hummers had appeared, no doubt called in by the soldiers once they had freed themselves. The crackle of a radio told her that they had fixed the radio Jacob had trashed.

Just as she got to within a hundred yards of the roadblock, one of the Hummers drove off. That left five soldiers standing in the road and perhaps more in the building.

Maybe some hiding in the dark too.

The roadblock was at a relatively straight portion of the road, with a steep slope going up on one side and down on the other. Jana got to the lower slope, where the soldiers would be less likely to post a sniper, and picked her way carefully past the roadblock and around behind the Land Rover. She could see all the doors were open. They had obviously searched it.

Had they found the secret compartments? If so, her mission was over before she had even started it.

In the half-light, she noticed a large rock on the downward slope not far from the rear of the vehicle. That would make a good firing position if she could make it there unnoticed. The soldiers were mostly just standing around now, two behind those body shields in front of the concrete bunkhouse, two more on the other side of the road, and one right next to the Land Rover, peering down the road.

How to do this? She had the advantage of surprise, but they outnumbered her at least five to one, and they could call for backup. That other Hummer was only a few minutes down the road. No bluffing this time. She had to stop them from getting to their radio. If only she had some stun grenades! And, she realized, with a sickening lurch in her gut, she couldn't afford to be nice. No shooting in the legs, no knocking people out. She had to shoot to kill, or Jacob and two other operatives would surely die.

God, how do I get myself into messes like this?

She got to the rock and braced her assault rifle. Her position lay just at the edge of the light, and they'd spot her pretty soon. She had to fire, and she had to fire now.

She aimed at the soldier by the Land Rover.

Sorry.

A single shot to the center mass. He doubled over and dropped. She pivoted her aim and took out one of the guys standing partially in sight behind the metal shield. She hit him in the helmet with a loud *clang*, his head whipping back, arms flying up, the man either knocked out or at least momentarily stunned.

The guy next to him ducked behind the bulletproof cover of his own shield, so Jana shifted aim to the two men near the building, who had dropped to one knee and had started to return fire, their bullets whizzing close overhead or snapping off the boulder she hid behind.

She got one, then had to duck for cover as the surviving man behind the metal shield sprayed her position on full auto. Hard to aim on full auto in poor light at that distance, but the sheer volume of bullets made it too dangerous to stay in sight.

Jana waited until the fire died down, then popped up on the other side of the boulder.

They had anticipated the move, however, and a new spray of bullets nearly took her head off.

Jana waited, heart hammering, ears throbbing from the gunfire, then came up in the exact same position.

They hadn't expected that, and it gave her a crucial half-second to aim at the man who remained exposed, running now for shelter in the building.

He didn't make it, Jana's bullet taking him in the thigh and dropping him. A spray of gunfire from the man behind the shield sent Jana ducking back into cover.

He must almost be out of ammo in his magazine.

Jana peeked and saw he had disappeared, concealed totally behind his shield. She saw a hint of movement behind the thick bulletproof glass near the top. Hard to see much through that stuff in poor light, for her or for him. She stayed as still as the stone she hid behind. Waiting.

He came around for another shot, and Jana took him out, the bullet tearing into his face and turning her stomach.

She paused, looking around at the destruction she had caused. The guy with the thigh wound was dragging himself toward the building. She thought she heard a groan from the man she hit in the helmet.

Jana decided to let them both live as compensation (such feeble compensation!) for the three she had killed.

Keeping an eye on them, she rushed over to the Land Rover and checked the back. The secret compartment had remained untouched. Inside lay the bulletproof case containing the laptop and satellite phone with its collapsible satellite dish. Next to it lay the compact package containing the shortwave transceiver, a spool of copper wire for an antenna, and a copper rod as a ground.

She took all of it and ran for the Hummer parked behind the building. As she did, the soldier she had wounded in the leg, who had made it to the doorway, suddenly turned over and pointed his gun at her.

Jana froze; her own gun was pointed at him. Their eyes met. She saw fear there and pain. She suspected he saw much the same thing.

For a moment, neither moved, neither fired. Then, slowly so as not to startle him, Jana put one foot in front of the other. He didn't fire. Jana kept moving, maintaining eye contact, finger on the trigger, until she had moved out of sight of the front door. Then she rushed to the Hummer, hopped in, and found the keys in the ignition.

Within moments she had sped off down the road.

***

Jacob had endured torture more than once in his career, but these guys really knew how to dish it out.

He was strapped to the medical table he had seen on his way to the cell, his wounded shoulder painfully and deliberately stretched out as far as it could reach. The bandage had been removed, and a butt end of a cigarette was stuck in the hole.

For the first hour, they had mostly used a cattle prod, giving him shock after shock that sent his muscles into convulsions and made his tender shoulder the center of all the pain in the universe.

He hadn't said a word about who he was or why he was there.

And they hadn't even asked. They seemed content for the moment to inflict pain, soften him up for the real interrogation later.

After some more electric shocks, along with the usual beatings and threats, a private had come into the room, whispered something into the ear of the lead interrogator, and they had all left.

Typical tactic. Leave him in suspense, dreading what might come next.

He used the time to slow his breathing, try to detach his mind to some other place, a safe place where they couldn't touch him. Zen meditation should have really been a part of his training. He could use some of that nonattachment stuff right about now.

Especially when he saw who they came back with.

Hussein ibn Hamza, one of the top operatives in the Sons of Imam Ali, the Afghanistan-based terror group that the new Balochi government was supporting.

A slim man of strikingly good looks, Hussein ibn Hamza could have easily been a fashion model if he had chosen a different path in life. He had the olive skin and big dark eyes that many women found attractive in Arab men and moved with the poise and grace of a dancer. Except for his gait. He had a slight limp thanks to a bullet Jacob had put in his leg a couple of years ago.

Hussein ibn Hamza was Saudi, although his own nation would never recognize him as such. The Shia minority in Saudi Arabia, indeed all Gulf States, was persecuted, passed over for any job of importance and insulted regularly in a thousand different ways.

Still, that was no excuse to blow up shopping malls or gun down pilgrims to Sunni holy sites. This guy and his group did that at every available opportunity.

"Jacob Snow, how good to see you again," Hussein ibn Hamza purred in perfect English.

"Hey, Hussein, how's the leg?"

"Better. Thank you for asking."

"Too bad I didn't shoot you in your pretty boy face."

"Lost opportunities, my friend, lost opportunities. I lost an opportunity to kill you when you stole Arash Mousavi from us." He leaned over Jacob, bringing his face close, those soft eyes growing hard. "I will not miss another chance."

"I suppose you want to know where we took your leader."

"Naturally."

"You think you can bust him out?"

"Perhaps. We can certainly kill many CIA operatives in the attempt."

"I'm not telling you crap."

Hussein ibn Hamza shook his head and smiled. "I certainly hope not, Mr. Snow. I don't want you to tell me. I want you to resist and keep on resisting, so that you can feel more pain. So much pain that it will eventually, some weeks from now, overcome you and your heart gives out. That's what I want. I want to spend a great deal of time with you, Mr. Snow, and I want you to give me the excuse to do so by telling me nothing."

CHAPTER TWENTY THREE

Jana rubbed her eyes and stifled a yawn as the midmorning sun shone down on the isolated gully she had hiked to after her Hummer could make it no further on the rough terrain the previous night. Then she keyed the mic and sent out the distress call for the hundredth time.

"313, this is Icarus. Northfield, Northfield, Northfield. Your student is in the same position I was in when you sent your last message. I repeat, your student is in the same position I was in when you sent your last message."

She stopped hitting the send key on the mic and listened to the crackle of static on the shortwave band. No response on this frequency or the other two she had tried and tried for so many hours.

Jana wished she knew more of the code her father and Jacob had used. The number 313 was the codename for her father, although it also had the meaning that he wasn't in a position to help. Icarus was the codename for herself. Northfield was a signal of distress. She didn't know the word for Jacob, so she just called him her dad's student.

She hoped that would be enough for whoever might be listening.

She had tried all the frequencies at the correct UTC times and also at the local time. Then she second-guessed herself and tried the frequencies one hour ahead and behind, in case they were using local time for other nearby time zones. Eventually, she just started broadcasting every hour at twenty minutes past, alternating between the three frequencies.

No luck, no answer, except from an angry ham radio operator in Australia who griped at her for speaking in code on an amateur radio band, which was "against international regulations."

Maybe it was for him, but she was in a situation that had gone far beyond any sort of regulations.

She got up to stretch her legs and drink a bit of water. Then she checked the antenna was in order, strung from the top of a rock to a cairn she had built to get the length of copper wire as high up as possible. Then she checked the car battery she was using for power. Yep, still had juice in it.

All was in order. She was transmitting, just no one was responding.

Maybe no one was listening.

She'd keep it up all day if she had to, and if she got no response, tonight she'd try to break into the prison.

Jana still had no plans on how to do that. She had an Army Hummer, an assault rifle, a water supply in the Hummer that would last her a couple of days, and no food. Her stomach had been growling for hours.

But she'd figure out a way. She had to.

***

A voice in the darkness. It keeps saying something. Something familiar. Over and over again.

It sounds patient as if it had spoken that strange word many times and knew that it would, in the end, have the effect it wanted.

The repeated word became clearer, pushing through the darkness. Now pain rose up, momentarily muting the word, but the voice continued its patient repetition.

"Jacob. Jacob. Wake up, Jacob."

Jacob? What did that mean?

"Come on, Jacob. You need to wake up."

That's my name. He's talking to me.

"Jacob."

Who is that?

The voice kept repeating, pushing through the pain.

"Jacob. You need to give me some indication you can hear me. Come on, Jacob."

Jacob let out a grunt. It hurt his throat and jaw.

"Good, Jacob. That's good. Do you know who I am?"

No.

"Answer me, Jacob."

With a supreme effort and agonizing pain, Jacob opened his mouth and said, "Jana?"

"Who? No. I'm not Jana. Think a minute."

"You're … " Instinct kicked in. "I … I shouldn't use your real name."

The effort to say one sentence exhausted Jacob so much he lapsed back into unconsciousness.

As the darkness closed in, he heard Robert say, "That's good, Jacob. You're brain doesn't seem to be affected. You get some rest."

***

Nightfall. Jana had barely waited until dark before she decided to set out, her throat hoarse from calling out on the radio over and over again. Still no answer. Maybe she was wrong about the fake phone numbers being shortwave frequencies. Maybe there was no one to hear her call. Feeling defeated, she had taken down the antenna, packed away the transmitter, replaced the car battery in the Hummer, and got ready to drive off down the bare rocky slope of the back hills to where she had fled.

Just then, a faint, familiar sound made her freeze—a phone ringing.

For a crazy moment, she thought it was her phone, although surely there was no coverage way out here.

Just as she reached for her pocket, she realized the sound had come from her campsite—it was the satellite phone. She had set up the dish beforehand, and its automatic tracker had kept it honed in on the spy satellite. She had been wracking her brain trying to figure out what the password might be so she could call for help.

She scrambled to get the clasps of the bulletproof case open. The phone lay inside next to the laptop. Timidly, she picked it up.

"Hello?" she said in English.

Silence.

She continued: "Hello, is this, um, Tyler Wallace?" Her heart leaped with hope. Finally, someone who could help!

"Who is this?" a male voice demanded.

"Um … "

"Who is this? How did you get access to this phone?"

"Is this Tyler Wallace?"

"Who is this?"

"Wait? Don't hang up! This is Jana Peters."

"Jana Peters! What are you doing there?"

"Don't be mad at Jacob. Mr. Wallace. I forced him to bring me along."

"*Forced* him?"

"Well, um, convinced him. We were on a mission in Morocco together."

As soon as the words slipped out of her mouth, Jana winced.

"What mission? He was on vacation!" the man bellowed.

Well, now that the cat's out of the bag ...

“We were investigating clues that my father might still be alive.”

Silence.

Wait. You’re not going to react to that?

Jana suddenly felt paralyzed—with fear, with hope, with anticipation.

Wallace’s answer came out level, toneless. “Why do you think he might be alive?”

“A coded phone call Jacob got when I was kidnapped in Mexico, alerting him to what had happened and using a personal code only known to him and my father.”

“I don’t see how that’s possible,” Wallace said, sounding confused. Real or fake confusion? She had caught him off guard, but now he might have gathered himself together.

Or maybe this was all fantasy on her part, and he really didn’t think Dad was alive. He’d be in the best position to know, right? Whatever the truth might be, he wasn’t going to tell her anything. He might not know himself, and if he did, he had had years to tell her the truth.

She didn’t have time to march wits with some CIA station director halfway around the world. Not with Jacob in prison.

“Look, I need your help,” Jana said. “Jacob has been captured. He’s in the same prison as Robert and Oscar. He left behind the satellite phone and the thumb drive, so the Balochis still don’t have any incriminating evidence about the original mission, but we got into a couple of firefights and now the Balochis have every reason in the world to parade them before the international media. We need to get him out of there before they do.”

There was a pause, then quietly, “Damn. I was afraid he’d pull something like this.”

“Sorry, but he couldn’t leave those two men behind. When is the rescue team coming? I can meet with them and give them some intel. I’ve already looked over the prison and the approaches to it.”

Another pause, longer this time. “There’s no rescue team coming.”

“What? I—”

“I wanted one, fought for one, but they’re still trying the diplomatic option.”

“That’s the one option that *won’t* work!”

“I know. I told them. The higher-ups won’t listen. The international situation is very delicate right now. The White House is nervous about making waves. And Jacob getting captured only makes the situation even more delicate. When I pass this on, the White House will go into diplomatic overdrive. We had plausible deniability up until now, but Jacob trying and failing to bust them out plays into the regional government's hands. His attack is proof that they were right all along."

Jana bit her lip. Everything he said was true. She and Jacob had been impulsive and had given the new regional government exactly what they wanted.

"If the pretense is gone, then we don't have anything to lose by sending a rescue team."

"No, that only compounds the problem. We're seen as meddling in a foreign state, one with a fragile central government. Plus we're also seen taking sides on the Shia and Sunni split."

"But one of those militant groups is making a dirty bomb! We can reveal that."

"Jesus! He told you that? No. If we show we know their operation, the group will move the radioactive materials. An airstrike is being planned as we speak. We'll take out the entire camp. But that leaves no evidence we can get to. We could present satellite and drone footage, but except to trained eyes it doesn't look like a smoking gun. The Balochis will still have deniability. We can't publicize the airstrike, and the Balochis and the central government will pretend it didn't happen. It's in everyone's best interest."

"What about Jacob's best interest? And Robert's? And Oscar's?"

"They knew the risks when they took them. Every agent takes on that responsibility for themselves."

Just like Dad.

"So you're leaving them to get tortured and killed."

"They won't kill them. They need them."

"Yeah, right."

"It's out of my hands. I'm sorry."

Something occurred to her.

"Wait. Why were you calling?"

Deep sigh. "To order him back to Karachi as soon as possible. I was worried he might do something like this. At first I thought it might not be a bad idea, because I knew it would kill him to walk away, but then I realized it would kill him to try, as well as screw up the political situation even more. So I changed my mind and hoped I could change his."

"I'm the one who pushed him into it," she admitted. "I was going to help him, but he ditched me."

"Did you fly with him from Morocco?"

"Yes."

"Then you already know Orhan Yildirim. He's waiting in Karachi, at the Nazimuddin Hotel. He'll fly you wherever you need to go."

"I appreciate that, but I'm not going anywhere."

"Ms. Peters, you might have received some training from your father, but you cannot break into a prison that's on high alert and has already captured three CIA agents."

"But I'm going to try."

"It's suicide! And you'll only be making matters worse."

"Do you want me to destroy the thumb drive before I make the attempt?"

"I want you to destroy the thumb drive and go straight to Karachi. You can't try and break him out!"

"I know the risks and I'm taking that responsibility on myself."

She hung up, took a deep breath, and looked around her at the darkening mountains. Pulling out the thumb drive, she dropped it on the ground and stomped on it with her boot until it was in several pieces.

Time to go. She packed up her gear, started the engine, and drove down the mountainside.

CHAPTER TWENTY FOUR

It was fully night now. The Humvee bounced over the rough terrain with its lights off. Jana was coming down a back route that wasn't a road, wasn't even a trail, but thankfully the Hummer was designed to get across rough ground like this. Jana kept her head out the open window in order to see better in the dark. She didn't dare turn her lights on.

As best she could estimate, Jana was a few kilometers behind the checkpoint they had attacked twice and would come down into the prison valley from a different angle.

From there, she planned to wait. Jacob had mentioned that the spy satellite intel showed that military vehicles came into the prison at all hours. She planned on waiting in the darkness until she saw some heading for the prison and then swept onto the road behind and joined them. There were surely enough patrols out in these mountains looking for her that it wouldn't look too out of place.

A dicey plan. What if they radioed her to identify herself? The radio in the Hummer had been crackling all night with messages back and forth. The whole region was on high alert.

And even if they didn't check by radio, they'd be sure to check her visually at the gate.

She'd have to blast her way through with only an assault rifle and some spare clips of ammo she'd found in the Hummer.

Wallace is right. This really is suicide.

But I can't leave him. Not if I want to call myself Aaron Peters' daughter.

Not if I want to call myself Jacob Snow's friend.

The Hummer itself could be a weapon, she tried to reassure herself. This one had been reinforced and fitted with bulletproof glass. It would protect her against any small arms fire the guards could throw her way. She could use it as a ram. Maybe she could break through the prison door once she'd found it.

All those plans disappeared a moment later when a fire erupted behind several boulders to her right.

The right side of her Humvee lit up with sparks as assault rifle rounds bounced off the armor, the sight disappearing from view as the bulletproof glass spiderwebbed, absorbing the shots but at the cost of a thousand little cracks to the compromised material.

Jana tried to pick up speed. She closed the driver's side window, thanking her luck that the ambush hadn't been on that side. She flicked on the lights so she could see better …

… just in time to spot the man with the RPG standing behind a cluster of rocks right in front of her.

She veered to the instant he fired.

The round took the Humvee in the back corner wheel and spun the vehicle around. It hit a rock on the slope and teetered on its side.

Jana rammed her body in the opposite direction, hoping her weight, puny as it was compared to the big vehicle, might be enough to right it.

For a sickening moment, the Hummer poised in the balance, then slowly toppled over on its side. Jana slammed against the door.

Shaking off her shock, she grabbed her assault rifle, popped open a door on the top side, and tried to climb out.

She had to drop back down immediately as a hail of bullets came in her direction. Several panged off the Hummer's undercarriage, near the vulnerable gas tank and gas lines. The vehicle could go up in a fireball at any moment.

Checking out the window, she saw the guy with the RPG reloading. Other soldiers closed in on all sides.

No way out, and if she stayed here, that RPG would blast right through the Humvee. It was nowhere near armored enough to resist a rocket-propelled grenade at this range.

The firing stopped. Through the open door, she heard a man shout in English.

"Surrender! Surrender and we don't kill you!"

Jana scrambled to the back of the Humvee, away from where the blast would come.

Once she got there, she stopped. What was the point? Assuming she didn't get killed from the blast, they'd rush in here and take her out.

Jana slumped. She had failed.

"Surrender! This is the last time I say it!"

Damn it.

She dropped her assault rifle and then poked first one hand, then the other out of the open door.

"Come out!"

She lifted herself out and found twenty men had surrounded the Hummer.

They closed in, smiling triumphantly.

***

The guards pushed her into a cell and slammed the door behind her. Once Jana picked herself off the floor, she saw the bloody heap in the corner and gasped.

"Jacob!"

She rushed over. His wounded shoulder was a mass of half-dried blood. The bandage and his shirt had been ripped away. His body was covered with burn marks and bruises, one eye swollen shut, and lips split.

Blearily, barely conscious, he turned his good eye but not his head in her direction. It widened.

"Jana," he rasped. "What happened? How did they catch you?"

"I went into the hills to try those radio frequencies. They didn't work. Then I came down to get you."

"You did what?"

"I couldn't leave you behind."

"Why didn't you bug out? You could have stolen a vehicle and been in Karachi by now!"

"I'm sorry, I had to."

Jacob groaned and sank back down. She wondered if she should tell him about the phone call with Wallace and decided against it. Too cruel.

It was bad enough knowing it herself. No help was coming. She'd be in for the same treatment Jacob had suffered, or worse.

"Did you at least destroy it?" he asked.

"Yes. Smashed into a million pieces."

"Thank God!" someone shouted from another cell.

"Who's that?" Jana asked.

"One of the guys you were trying to save. You shouldn't have tried, whoever you are, but thank you."

"Did they get the laptop and satellite phone?" Jacob asked.

Jana hung her head. "Yes. I'm sorry. I should have destroyed that too."

"Don't worry. While it looks suspicious as hell, there's no memory on that thing. There's nothing to access even if they hack the password."

"Good," Jana said, letting out a gust of air. At least she hadn't screwed up entirely. "That's good."

Footsteps down the hall. Jana turned toward the door, feeling a chill. Were they coming for her already?

The door opened. A slim man who looked to be from the Gulf stood there, flanked by two soldiers with their guns leveled.

"Hello. You must be a friend of Jacob's. I'm a longtime acquaintance of his. Allow me to introduce myself. I am Hussein ibn Hamza. I am an officer in the Sons of Imam Ali, a group Jacob tried and failed to destroy. He has killed many of our brothers, though, and captured our leader. I've been working on him for quite some time, as you can see, but he hasn't given up the location where they're keeping him."

"He'll never tell you anything!" Jana snapped.

Hussein ibn Hamza shrugged. "No, not before you showed up. But now? I think things have changed now. I'm thinking that if I work on you instead of him, that might be just the thing to make him break."

Jacob tried to fling himself toward the door but only managed to flop forward a couple of feet before landing hard on the concrete floor with a groan. The guards laughed.

"Think about it, Jacob. I could do all sorts of horrible things to her. You've seen our videos. We can be quite creative. But first I think I'll give her to the guards. They won't be creative at all. They'll do just what you and I know they will do."

"Bastard," Jacob mumbled through swollen lips.

"I'll give you an hour to think about it. When I come back, the answer had better be yes, otherwise you'll get to watch as we destroy this American woman's soul."

He turned and went out. The door slammed shut.

Jana shuddered. After a moment, she helped Jacob get back on the musty old sleeping bag that served as a bed.

He gestured for her to get closer.

"The hem of my left sock," he whispered.

Jana blinked, then reached down and examined the hem of his sock. They had taken his boots, and there were spots of blood on the white cotton. As she felt around the hem, she came on something hard, about half the size of a pill. She tore at the material with her nail until she could get it out.

It was a tiny capsule. She didn't need to be told what was inside. Jacob gestured for her to get close again.

"For you," he whispered. "Before he comes back."

Jana licked her lips, which had suddenly gone dry, and looked from Jacob to the capsule and back to Jacob again.

"You should have it," she whispered.

"No. Take it." He managed a smile, blood oozing from the wound on his lips. "It's not exactly a bouquet of roses, but I realized I've never given you anything."

Jana's heart softened. "You've given me the chance to make a difference. What more could you give me? And you've made me realize just what Dad was up against. I've forgiven him now. Thank you."

Jacob closed his eyes, exhausted. "I'm glad." He opened them suddenly. "Before you take it, I have something else to tell you."

"What's that?"

"I love you."

Jana took his hand, tears filling her eyes.

"I love you too, Jacob."

CHAPTER TWENTY FIVE

Esirk Umrani lit another cigarette and looked out over the prison yard from his perch in one of the guard towers. It had been a crazy few days. First, the special forces had captured two foreign spies and their Pakistani lackeys, then some mad foreigner had tried to break into prison to free them.

Incredible. No one had ever managed to come close to breaking out of this bit of hell on earth, and here was this spy trying to break in.

He hadn't gotten far, Esirk thought with a chuckle as he breathed in the smoke.

They'd been on high alert ever since, waiting for another attempt. Esirk didn't think there'd be one because the spy had come alone. Probably he had been part of their team and had eluded the initial capture. Esirk had assumed no one else would make an attempt.

But then they brought in a foreign woman, probably the lover of one of the three spies or all of them. Foreign women were loose. Just look at how they dressed! And he had heard they would sleep with men before they got married, and Western men saw nothing wrong with this. Imagine marrying a woman who wasn't a virgin!

Still, he thought, giving the prison block an uneasy look, she didn't deserve what would happen to her in there. The men in the interrogation unit were sick in their minds. Sure, a spy needed to be roughed up until they talked, but the freaks who worked in the prison block basement actually enjoyed giving pain. He'd heard them brag and laugh in the canteen and show off pictures they had taken on their phones.

Esirk had always looked away when they did that. They mocked him for being weak, but he didn't care. He didn't want approval from men like that, men who were thrilled at the sight of blood and the anguished faces of helpless victims strapped down and brought to the edge of their endurance.

He was a soldier, and he wanted a soldier's life. He would love it if his government declared independence from Islamabad. Then he could go to the front line and fight for his people. A soldier fighting other soldiers in an honorable fashion. Instead, the politicians fiddled about, trying to get concessions from the central government and line their own pockets in the process.

Instead, he found himself watching over terrified, helpless men while beasts who wore the same uniform as he did take pleasure in their suffering.

This was not what he had enlisted for. It gave him nightmares, and he worried that God would judge him for the company he kept. Didn't the Koran say not to keep company with sinners?

But what could he do? He couldn't leave. He had a year left on his service. If he tried to leave, he'd end up as one of the poor souls in the prisoners' block.

Esirk remembered the last prisoner they had dragged out to dump in the desert. A Balochi thief and murderer, and while he had surely lived a sinful life, he hadn't deserved to have his body shattered or to be left in the desert without a Muslim burial to be picked at by crows.

The sound of footsteps made him turn. Jafar was coming up the spiral staircase of the guard tower, having visited the cesspit that passed for a toilet in this miserable place. Esirk took another drag of his cigarette. There seemed not to be enough cigarettes in the world to get him to relax.

Jafar appeared, looking as tired as Esirk felt. He was twenty-two, the same age as Esirk, and had joined the army out of the same sense of patriotism.

"Still here?" he asked. The old joke.

"Haven't jumped the wall yet."

"I was tempted to try and swim through the plumbing and then remembered I couldn't swim." Jafar lit a cigarette. "I was going to light up on the toilet, but there was so much gas in the air I was afraid of blowing the place up."

Esirk chuckled and looked out over the prison yard, lit by harsh floodlights that burned his eyes and blanked out the beautiful stars he so enjoyed looking at back in his village. No movement, except for the other pairs of soldiers at the towers on each corner of the compound and the pair of soldiers at the gate. Turning, he looked out over the desert, black outside the reach of the floodlights, the mountains all around merely hints of shadows.

"I got to get out of here," Esirk murmured.

Jafar put a hand on his shoulder. "Only one more year. Then you can go back to your village and the matchmaker will find you a nice girl. You can farm your family's land and raise good sons."

Jafar grunted. Some day.

A flicker of movement out of the corner of his eye caught his attention. He turned to the northeast tower at the back side of the compound. Neither of the two men on duty stood there.

Idiots probably decided to take a nap. They better not let Captain Dashti catch them.

Then a realization chilled his heart.

They were there just a minute ago.

"What is it?" Jafar asked.

"I'm not sure," Esirk said.

Esirk glanced around the compound. Everyone else was at their posts. He turned back to the northeast guard tower. Still no one in sight.

He grabbed the walkie talkie lying on a shelf next to his and Jafar's helmets. While they were supposed to wear their helmets on duty, not even Captain Dashti insisted on that. Wearing a big bowl of Kevlar on your head for six hours of sentry duty was too much to ask. Even during that break-in attempt, they hadn't needed them.

He keyed the walkie talkie to life. "Northeast tower, this is southeast tower. Everything all right over there?"

No response.

"Northeast tower. Answer, please."

Answer before you get in trouble, idiots. An officer might be listening.

"Northeast tower, are you—"

Every floodlight, both outside and inside the prison yard, suddenly went dark. Lights still shone from the barracks windows, and from a couple of small windows in the prison block, but most of the yard was now shrouded in shadow.

"What happened?" Jafar cried.

Suddenly the walkie talkie crackled with a jumble of voices, all asking the same thing.

Esirk crouched down, peeking over the parapet of the guard tower and revealing himself as little as possible.

The door at the base of the northeast tower, leading into the central yard, opened. A figure flitted along the shadows, barely visible.

"Look out!" Esirk said, clutching his assault rifle.

The flare of a gun barrel. Jafar flew back. He hit the other side of the parapet, tipped over, and was gone.

Esirk cursed and ducked down.

More shots. The thud of a grenade. Esirk crawled over to the shelf and put on his helmet. Then he peeked back over the lip of the parapet.

A bullet found him instantly, panging off his helmet, and jerking his head back. He found himself lying on the floor, his head ringing.

***

Jana held Jacob's hand, the cyanide pill in her other hand. She gazed into Jacob's eyes.

"I want you to take it," Jana said. "It was given to you."

"No. Please take it yourself. You don't know this guy. I've seen his videos."

"I can imagine," Jana said, her throat dry.

"No, you can't. Please take it. As a last gift to me. I can't stand to watch you go through that."

"A last gift to you? I never gave you anything."

Jacob squeezed her hand. It killed her to feel how weak his grip was. "You gave me more than you can know."

A loud bang in the hallway outside. For a moment, Jana thought it was some other cell door opening, but it sounded duller, deeper, like an explosion.

Then came the unmistakable sounds of gunfire.

It lasted only a moment.

Jana scrambled to the door and peeked through the slit where meals were shoved through. She could see nothing except a stretch of hallway.

The click of a lock. A door opening. Robert's voice.

"Whoever you are, I sure am glad to see you!"

"Take this gun," a male voice said.

Jana's heart froze. That sounded like …

… no, it couldn't be. Impossible.

A pair of booted feet appeared in front of her cell door. Jana gasped and backed up, getting to her feet and moving to Jacob's side, hand poised to pop the cyanide capsule into her mouth.

The lock clicked. The door creaked open. In the hallway stood a tall, lean figure, a black headscarf wrapped around his head and the lower part of his face.

Jana gasped. She couldn't quite believe what she was seeing.

He reached up to the side of his head and unfastened the headscarf, allowing the portion around his face to drop, revealing his features.

Aaron Peters, her lost-lost father, stood there.

Even though she had given him up for dead years ago, and she felt like she was seeing a ghost, it was unmistakably him. The same tall, muscular frame. The same close-cropped brown hair peppered with gray. The same rugged face crisscrossed with old scars and a couple of new ones. The same sharp gray eyes softened as they saw her.

Jana leaped into his arms, all the long years of resentment and condemnation falling away.

***

Esirk Umrani, his head throbbing, trembled in his hiding place as he heard the gunfire erupt once again.

He had to do his duty. He had to get back into the fight. They had killed Jafar, and what had Jafar ever done to anyone?

Except for work in this horrible place, like I have. God is bringing his judgment down on us for standing by while evil happened.

He peeked over the parapet of his guard tower.

Bodies lay scattered across the prison yard. Both sentries by the gate lay dead. A cluster of his comrades hid at one end of the barracks, watching the prison door.

It was wide open.

The soldiers didn't dare chase the intruder inside the prison. They were waiting for him to come out and ambush him when he did.

Esirk readied his assault rifle and aimed at the entrance, his mouth dry, muscles tense.

He waited, the seconds stretching to hours.

Then he noticed something. His finger wasn't on the trigger. It was on the trigger guard.

Nerves? He had never made that mistake before. He had even gotten a commendation for being the best shot in his regiment.

He shifted his finger and stopped halfway through the movement.

What are you doing? Get ready!

He didn't want to. No matter what the prisoners had done, none of them—the killers, the thieves, the spies—none of them deserved what they got in there.

He tried to put his finger on the trigger, but something stopped him.

The intruder thinks you're dead up here. You can surprise him. You can be a hero.

A hero for whom? A government that allows a place like this to exist?

A streak of light from the prison door crossed the darkened prison yard to slam into the corner of the barracks where the soldiers hid.

A blinding explosion enveloped them all. Esirk hunkered down lower behind the parapet.

The group of foreigners burst out of the front door of the prison. Leading them was a man Esirk could tell right off was an elite fighter. The way he moved, the way he carried himself. Coming behind were the two original spies, one carrying the other, while that Pakistani university student limped by their side.

Taking up the rear came the foreign woman, carrying the first intruder. He looked terrible, practically dead.

He felt a deep relief to see the woman did not look the same.

Now. None of them see you.

Esirk widened his stance to get into position, raised his assault rifle, and aimed at the man in the lead.

They rushed to one of the Humvees while the Pakistani student limped to the gate to hit the button and open it.

Esirk trained his rifle on the lead man, the one who had burst in here minutes before and killed so many. He had him in his sights. An easy shot. A single pull of the trigger and he'd be dead. And the others would get caught and go back to their cells.

Esirk eased his finger away from the trigger, knelt down behind the parapet, and closed his eyes. He listened as the gate hummed open, a few more shots rang out, and one of the Humvees started up and drove away, the rumble of its engine fading away into the distance.

Esirk Umrani felt the dent in his helmet and knew he could use that as an excuse for why he hadn't done his duty. But he had done his duty. A higher duty. And he hoped that those strange foreigners, whatever their crimes, would make it out of Pakistan safely.

NOW AVAILABLE!

TARGET SIX
(The Spy Game—Book #6)

"Thriller writing at its best... A gripping story that's hard to put down."
--Midwest Book Review, Diane Donovan (re Any Means Necessary)

"One of the best thrillers I have read this year. The plot is intelligent and will keep you hooked from the beginning. The author did a superb job creating a set of characters who are fully developed and very much enjoyable. I can hardly wait for the sequel."
--Books and Movie Reviews, Roberto Mattos (re Any Means Necessary)

From #1 bestselling and USA Today bestselling author Jack Mars, author of the critically acclaimed *Luke Stone* and *Agent Zero* series (with over 5,000 five-star reviews), comes an explosive new action-packed espionage series that takes readers on a wild ride across Europe, America, and the world.

After a brazen theft from the basement of the Louvre, a terrorist organization holds a mysterious, un-catalogued relic for ransom. When a pyramid is destroyed—and hundreds killed—the stakes escalate, with other high-profile targets—and civilian lives—in their sights. With lives on the line, Jacob Snow, elite soldier-turned-CIA agent, must team up with his mysterious archeologist partner to figure out what they stole, who they are—and how to stop them before it's too late.

An unputdownable action thriller with heart-pounding suspense and unforeseen twists, TARGET SIX is the sixth novel in an exhilarating new series by a #1 bestselling author that will make you fall in love with a brand-new action hero—and keep you turning pages late into the night. Perfect for fans of Dan Brown, Daniel Silva and Jack Carr.

Future books in the series are now available.

Jack Mars

Jack Mars is the USA Today bestselling author of the LUKE STONE thriller series, which includes seven books. He is also the author of the new FORGING OF LUKE STONE prequel series, comprising six books; of the AGENT ZERO spy thriller series, comprising twelve books; of the TROY STARK thriller series, comprising five books; and of the SPY GAME thriller series, comprising seven books.

Jack loves to hear from you, so please feel free to visit www.Jackmarsauthor.com to join the email list, receive a free book, receive free giveaways, connect on Facebook and Twitter, and stay in touch!

BOOKS BY JACK MARS

THE SPY GAME
TARGET ONE (Book #1)
TARGET TWO (Book #2)
TARGET THREE (Book #3)
TARGET FOUR (Book #4)
TARGET FIVE (Book #5)
TARGET SIX (Book #6)
TARGET SEVEN (Book #7)

TROY STARK THRILLER SERIES
ROGUE FORCE (Book #1)
ROGUE COMMAND (Book #2)
ROGUE TARGET (Book #3)
ROGUE MISSION (Book #4)
ROGUE SHOT (Book #5)

LUKE STONE THRILLER SERIES
ANY MEANS NECESSARY (Book #1)
OATH OF OFFICE (Book #2)
SITUATION ROOM (Book #3)
OPPOSE ANY FOE (Book #4)
PRESIDENT ELECT (Book #5)
OUR SACRED HONOR (Book #6)
HOUSE DIVIDED (Book #7)

FORGING OF LUKE STONE PREQUEL SERIES
PRIMARY TARGET (Book #1)
PRIMARY COMMAND (Book #2)
PRIMARY THREAT (Book #3)
PRIMARY GLORY (Book #4)
PRIMARY VALOR (Book #5)
PRIMARY DUTY (Book #6)

AN AGENT ZERO SPY THRILLER SERIES
AGENT ZERO (Book #1)
TARGET ZERO (Book #2)

HUNTING ZERO (Book #3)
TRAPPING ZERO (Book #4)
FILE ZERO (Book #5)
RECALL ZERO (Book #6)
ASSASSIN ZERO (Book #7)
DECOY ZERO (Book #8)
CHASING ZERO (Book #9)
VENGEANCE ZERO (Book #10)
ZERO ZERO (Book #11)
ABSOLUTE ZERO (Book #12)

Made in United States
North Haven, CT
16 June 2024